Immortals Code

OrangeBooks Publication

1st Floor, Rajhans Arcade, Mall Road, Kohka, Bhilai, Chhattisgarh 490020

Website: **www.orangebooks.in**

First Edition, 2025

ISBN: 978-93-7426-338-9

Price: Rs. 299.00

Printed in India

IMMORTALS CODE

KULDEEP SINGH SALUJA

OrangeBooks Publication
www.orangebooks.in

In loving memory of my Nani,

whose stories shaped my dreams,

whose teachings shaped my life,

and whose love shaped my heart —

my first teacher, my storyteller, my forever love.

Author's Note

Immortals Code began as a simple thought:

What if ancient mythology and modern science were never separate worlds?

What if they were always connected—coded into us?

This story grew from that question, shaped by the legends I heard growing up, the wisdom passed down by my elders, and the curiosity that has followed me all my life. The characters in this book—Rishab, Reet, Roshan, and even the dark paths of K.A.L-13 and Kalrakt—carry pieces of the stories we all grew up with, but seen through a new lens:

a world where meditation meets machinery, destiny meets technology, and time itself becomes both a weapon and a teacher.

Writing this book has been a journey of rediscovery for me.

Rediscovering our mythology.

Rediscovering imagination.

Rediscovering the power of belief—both ancient and futuristic.

If you find moments in these pages that remind you of childhood tales, if you feel the thrill of stepping into unknown worlds, or if you simply lose yourself for a while in this blend of myth and sci-fi, then this book has done what it was meant to do.

Thank you for stepping into this journey with me.

Now, it is time to enter the world of Immortals Code.

— Kuldeep Singh Saluja

Content

Chapter 1

The Breath Between Worlds

In year 2077, The sun had barely crested the horizon, its light diffused by the thick, lush canopy of the ancient jungle. This far from the touch of human civilization, nature reigned supreme. The towering trees, wrapped in moss and vines, stretched toward the heavens. The air was rich with the smell of damp earth, tinged with the fragrance of blooming flowers. Birds began their morning chorus, while the distant waterfall rumbled like a divine hymn, a constant reminder of the eternal flow of life.

It was in this serene, sacred environment that Rishab had chosen to live, far from the distractions of the modern world. For years, he had embraced a life of solitude, dedicated solely to his pursuit of moksha, the ultimate liberation from the cycle of birth, death, and rebirth. Every day, he woke before the sun, his body naturally attuned to the rhythms of the earth. His long, unkempt hair fell freely around his shoulders, his beard thick and wild, but his face radiated an inner calm born of years of intense spiritual discipline.

Rishab sat cross-legged on the forest floor, his spine erect, hands resting gently on his knees, palms facing upward. His breath was slow, deep, and measured, a practiced rhythm that had become second nature. In his mind, there was silence—a quiet, empty space cultivated through years of meditation. His eyes were closed, not in sleep, but in deep focus. He was fully awake, though his thoughts had long since stilled, leaving only the awareness of being.

This was his daily routine. Every morning, without fail, Rishab would rise before dawn and immerse himself in meditation. For hours, he would sit, unmoving, as his consciousness expanded beyond the confines of his physical body. This practice, this discipline, was the core of his life. It was the foundation upon which he built his quest for moksha.

Moksha—ultimate freedom from *samsara*, the cycle of life and death—had been his singular goal for as long as he could remember. The idea of liberation, of transcending the material world and merging with the infinite, had called to him since he was a young man. In pursuit of this, he had renounced the comforts of society, abandoned his family, and taken to the wilderness, where the distractions of the mundane world could not reach him. Here, in the heart of the jungle, he had found peace, or at least, the semblance of it.

As the first rays of sunlight pierced the canopy, dappled light danced on the ground around him, but Rishab remained unmoved. His breath, his *prana*, flowed through him in perfect harmony with the universe. He could feel the life force in the earth beneath him, in the trees around him, in the air he breathed. Each inhale brought him closer to unity with all things; each exhale was a release of ego, of attachment, of desire.

Today, however, something was different.

A subtle shift in the energy around him caused his breath to falter, if only for a moment. His heart, usually so steady, quickened slightly. It was as if the very air had thickened, becoming charged with an unseen force. Rishab's mind, usually so still, became aware of something stirring deep within him. For years, he had meditated, reaching ever closer to that elusive state of moksha, where the self dissolves into the cosmic ocean of existence. There had been moments when he felt on the verge of breaking free, when the veil between the material and the eternal seemed thin, almost transparent. But today was different. Today, something tugged at him, something beyond his control.

His breath hitched again. The delicate rhythm he had cultivated faltered, if only for an instant, but it was enough to break his meditation. Rishab opened his eyes, blinking against the sunlight that filtered through the trees. His heart was still racing, though his body remained perfectly still. The sensation was unlike anything he had experienced before. It wasn't fear—Rishab had long since conquered fear—but there was a sense of anticipation, of something immense and unknowable approaching from the depths of his being.

Rishab (in thought):

I am close. I feel the edge of something... more.

He closed his eyes once more, but this time, his meditation was different. The tranquility that usually enveloped him was gone, replaced by a current of energy that seemed to vibrate within him. It was as if the jungle around him had receded into the background, leaving only the pulse of life—the pulse of existence itself—echoing through his body. Rishab's breath deepened, his mind slipping from the physical world, expanding outward, beyond the boundaries of his skin, his flesh, his bones.

He was drifting, weightless, his consciousness no longer anchored to his body. The jungle sounds faded, replaced by a distant hum that seemed to emanate from within his own mind. The feeling was overwhelming, intoxicating, and yet, there was something else, too. A pull, an invisible force drawing him deeper into this state of awareness, as if some ancient power was awakening within him.

Rishab (in thought):

Am I ready? After all these years, am I truly prepared to leave this world behind?

The question lingered in his mind, unspoken but potent. For years, he had believed that he sought moksha—that he had prepared himself for the dissolution of self, the ultimate liberation. But now, standing at the threshold, doubt began to creep in. Had he truly understood what moksha meant? What lay beyond the veil of reality he had spent his life seeking to penetrate?

As his thoughts churned, a new sensation washed over him. It was as if the very air around him thickened, charged with energy. His skin prickled, and for the first time in years, he felt a presence—something outside of himself. His breath quickened, but not from fear. No, this was something else entirely. It was awe, a realization that something far greater than himself was unfolding.

Then, from the depths of the void, a voice emerged. It was not a voice like any he had ever heard. It did not come through his ears but resonated from every direction at once, vibrating through his very being.

Mysterious Voice (Immortal Ashwatthama):

"It is time, Rishab. The chosen one must awaken."

The words echoed within him, their meaning reverberating in his soul. Rishab's eyes snapped open, but he saw nothing of the jungle around him. The world he knew was gone. In its place was an endless void, a swirling mass of light and energy, a place where time and space held no meaning. His body, once so solid and real, now felt like little more than a shadow, a faint memory of his earthly existence.

Ashwatthama. The cursed warrior, burdened with immortality, wandering the earth as a symbol of divine punishment. Rishab had heard of him in ancient scriptures, but never had he imagined encountering him. His voice carried with it the weight of endless suffering and wisdom beyond mortal comprehension.

Voice of Vibhishana:

"You have carried the burden of life alone for many years, Rishab. But know this—you are not alone in your pursuit."

Rishab's breath caught as the voice surrounded him, different from the first yet just as ancient and powerful.

The realization dawned that these voices were not mere phantoms of his mind. These were the voices of the immortals—the Chiranjivi—those who had transcended the boundaries of time and death. Their presence filled him with both awe and a strange comfort. Vibhishana, the noble brother of Mokshaa who had embraced righteousness over familial loyalty, now spoke directly to him.

Voice of Vyasa:

"The pursuit of moksha is but one path. You have been called to something greater."

The swirling energy around him pulsed with life as another presence emerged. This time it was the great sage Vyasa, the compiler of the Vedas and author of the Mahabharata. His voice was calm, steady, like the flow of a river—timeless and wise. Vyasa's words resonated deep within Rishab, stirring something in him that went beyond his personal desires for liberation.

Voice of Parashurama:

"The time for meditation is over, Rishab. The world needs your strength. The awakening is not just for you—it is for all creation."

The force of Parashurama's voice was like the clash of thunder, sudden and undeniable. Rishab felt the weight of his message immediately. Parashurama, the warrior-sage who had destroyed entire Kshatriya lineages and yet, was a protector of dharma, now commanded him to rise. There was no longer time for passive pursuit. His quest for moksha was now intertwined with a larger destiny.

Rishab felt the weight of the words settle upon him like a mantle. His quest for moksha had been personal, an individual journey of liberation. But now, standing in the presence of the immortals, he realized that his path was intertwined with something much larger. His awakening was not merely his own—it was connected to the very fabric of existence.

Rishab (in thought):

This is it. The moment I have waited for. But why now?

Before the question could fully form, yet another voice, firm and commanding, resonated through the void.

Voice of Hanuman:

"Do not doubt, Rishab. You have been chosen because you are ready. Doubt will only delay the inevitable. Embrace your destiny."

The words struck Rishab with the force of a thousand storms. Hanuman's voice carried the wisdom of the ages, the strength of someone who had served righteousness for eons. His words left no room for uncertainty. Hanuman, the devoted servant of Lord Rishaba, was revered for his unshakable faith and loyalty. His presence alone filled Rishab with newfound courage, erasing any lingering hereettion.

Voice of Bali:

"In surrender, you will find your true strength. We, too, have walked the path of destiny, and now it is your turn."

The final voice was calm but resolute, like the steady rhythm of the waterfall he had once heard in the jungle. It was the voice of Bali, the king who had surrendered everything, yet remained immortal by the grace of Vishnu. His words offered guidance, not just for the moment but for the journey ahead. Bali's sacrifice had earned him a place among the immortals, a reminder that surrender, too, could lead to a greater truth.

Kripacharya's Voice:

"Your time in isolation has ended. The path you must walk is no longer one of solitude."

Kripacharya, the ancient preceptor of the Kauravas, now entered the chorus. His voice was calm but filled with authority, a teacher guiding a student at the cusp of transformation. Rishab had been in isolation for so long, seeking only his own enlightenment. But now, the truth revealed itself. He was not meant to walk the path alone any longer. He was being called to something beyond his personal journey—a role that required him to emerge from solitude and embrace a destiny that stretched beyond himself.

Rishab (in thought):

I was never alone. The universe has been guiding me here.

The realization settled deep within him. His years of solitude, his quest for moksha, had prepared him for this moment. But now, standing on the precipice of a new journey, he realized that his awakening was not just for his own enlightenment. The immortals had guided him here for a reason. They had awakened him because the world needed him—needed his strength, his wisdom, and his dedication.

Moksha was no longer his only goal. His life, which he had believed was meant to dissolve into the eternal, now had a purpose beyond his own liberation. The immortals had awakened him for a reason—a reason that stretched far beyond his individual enlightenment. The voice was right.

He had to awaken.

Rishab's spirit, once seeking only freedom from the world, now felt the weight of responsibility, of destiny. The voice had called him, and he knew he could not turn back. His path was clear. With a final, deep breath, Rishab closed his eyes once more, surrendering to the vast, infinite energy that surrounded him. The jungle, the world, his past—all of it faded into the background as he stepped fully into the unknown.

He was ready to awaken.

Chapter 2

When the Gods Whispered

Rishab's senses spun violently as he was pulled from the earthly plane, his body left far behind in the jungle. The world he had known—the verdant wilderness, the rustle of leaves, the distant roar of waterfalls—vanished. Instead, he was consumed by a sensation unlike anything he had experienced before. His consciousness, already expanded beyond the limits of his physical form, soared through an endless expanse of light and energy. Time itself bent and twisted around him. The familiar tether of gravity, which had always anchored him to the material world, disappeared, leaving him floating in a place where the rules of reality no longer applied.

He was no longer in the jungle.

The **Immortal Realm** unfolded before him, and the very sight of it defied understanding.

Rishab (in thought):

This... this is beyond anything I have ever known.

He hovered in awe, suspended in a reality that seemed to exist outside time. **Islands of stone** floated in the air, suspended in the void like forgotten fragments of ancient worlds. Some were massive, with entire forests and ruins perched upon them, while others were small, no larger than a single stone, drifting aimlessly. The sky—or what Rishab assumed was the sky—was a swirling tapestry of colors, constantly shifting between **gold, silver, and deep hues of violet**. Rivers of light, radiant and ethereal, cascaded between the islands, flowing **upward instead of down**, defying gravity. The rivers illuminated everything with a soft, otherworldly glow, casting long shadows that seemed to dance in the air.

Even the air was alive with energy, humming with a primordial force, ancient and powerful. It felt as though the very space around him thrummed with knowledge that spanned eons, far beyond anything human comprehension could grasp. Every breath Rishab took seemed to resonate with the hum, filling his being with a sense of deep, infinite wisdom.

He was standing—or perhaps floating—on one of these islands. Though there was no ground beneath his feet in the traditional sense, he felt somehow anchored, grounded in the weightlessness all around him. In the distance, **massive crystalline structures** stretched up toward the heavens, their forms spiraling and twisting in ways that seemed impossible. These structures glistened like diamonds, each facet reflecting the brilliant rivers of light flowing around them. The structures pulsed, as if they were alive, their rhythm seemingly synced with the very beat of Rishab's heart.

Rishab (in thought):

Am I truly here? Is this a dream? Or have I transcended the material world?

Before Rishab could fully comprehend the magnitude of the **Immortal Realm**, the air around him began to shift once more. The familiar hum intensified, and suddenly, a presence filled the space—**vast, overwhelming, and unmistakably divine**. The very fabric of the realm seemed to vibrate as it responded to the arrival of something far greater.

Rishab turned, and before him stood **seven towering figures**, each one radiant with an ancient power. These were no ordinary beings. They were the **Chiranjivi**, the **Seven Immortals**, who had transcended the boundaries of time and death. Their forms were both human and otherworldly, their appearances shifting like the landscapes around them. Each radiated a unique energy, as if they embodied both the physical and spiritual planes simultaneously. They wore flowing robes that shimmered with **symbols of the past and future**, their eyes glowing with an ancient wisdom that spanned eons.

Rishab had heard of these Immortals before, in the sacred texts and whispers of the wise. But never had he imagined he would stand before them, much less in a place beyond time and space.

Immortal 1 (Ashwatthama):

"The future is not what you think, Rishab. It is filled with destruction and pain. Moksha has bent time to his will. He must be stopped."

The voice of **Ashwatthama**, the cursed warrior of ancient legend, resonated deeply within Rishab. Ashwatthama's presence was commanding, but there was a sorrow that weighed heavily on him. He was a man who had been condemned to wander the earth eternally, never to find peace. His words echoed not only in the air, but within Rishab's very mind, as though they were woven into the fabric of existence itself.

Rishab's heart raced. He stared at the **Seven Immortals** in awe, unable to speak. These beings were far beyond anything he had encountered in his years of meditation and spiritual exploration. They were the very essence of both **myth and reality**, of both **magic and technology**. It was as if they were part of the very cosmos itself, beyond time, watching over the eternal flow of existence.

Another figure stepped forward. His presence was both gentle and resolute. **Vibhishana**, the brother of Mokshaa who had chosen righteousness over loyalty to his blood, gazed at Rishab with deep concern.

Immortal 2 (Vibhishana):

"Moksha seeks to undo the past to rebuild a future in his image. He is playing with time itself. You are the only one who can stop him."

The name **Moksha** struck a chord deep within Rishab. The mere mention of the name tugged at the edges of his mind, bringing forth distant, fragmented memories—shadows of battles fought in another life, another time. He saw flashes of a man, **consumed by power**, a man who had once been a great king but had fallen prey to ambition and darkness.

Rishab's mind raced, trying to piece together the scattered fragments of his memories. There was something disturbingly familiar about **Moksha**, as if he had encountered him before across the ages, but the details were just beyond his reach, slipping away like water through his fingers.

Rishab (in thought):

Moksha... I have encountered him before. But how?

As if in response to Rishab's confusion, the **Seven Immortals** reached out, and the air around them shimmered with a soft, radiant light. Suddenly, the space was filled with visions—**glimpses of a world ravaged by time**. Cities, once magnificent, now lay in ruins. Their once-glorious skyscrapers were reduced to rubble, their foundations cracked and broken. The oceans churned violently, **boiling under darkened skies** filled with ash and flame. The very **earth seemed to cry out in pain**, twisted and broken by forces beyond comprehension.

At the center of it all stood **Moksha**. He was no longer just a man—he was something far more dangerous. He stood before a monstrous machine, an unholy amalgamation of **cold steel and ancient magic**. Tubes filled with **glowing liquid—immortal blood**—fed into the machine, powering it. The machine crackled with energy, warping the air around it, creating a rift in time itself. Rishab watched in horror as Moksha activated the machine, the very fabric of reality bending to his will.

Immortal 3 (Vyasa):

"The future is lost unless you stop him.

You have fought him before, across many lifetimes, but this time will be different."

The vision faded, leaving Rishab standing once again in the glowing light of the Immortal Realm. His mind reeled from what he had seen. **Moksha**, the ancient enemy, was not just seeking to rule a kingdom. He was trying to **manipulate time itself**, to reshape the future in his own image. The thought was terrifying.

Rishab had spent his life seeking **moksha**, liberation from the cycle of birth and death, seeking peace and detachment from the material world. And yet, here he was, being told that his destiny was not to escape the material world, but to **save it**. The enormity of the task weighed heavily on him. How could he—a man who had only ever sought peace—be the one to stop such a cataclysm?

Rishab (in thought):

I never asked for this. I only wanted to transcend...

But the Immortals were not finished. Another stepped forward, his presence filled with strength and wisdom. It was **Hanuman**, the beloved servant of Lord Rishaba, the eternal protector and warrior. Hanuman's presence radiated both kindness and power, his eyes glowing with divine purpose.

Immortal 4 (Hanuman):

"This time, Moksha is stronger than before. He seeks to control the very fabric of time itself. You must awaken the strength within you, Rishab. The world depends on it."

Hanuman's voice reverberated through the space, carrying with it the weight of an eternal protector's burden. Rishab felt a surge of both **hope and fear**. Hanuman had faced Mokshaa before, during the ancient battles of old. If even **Hanuman** believed the danger was greater now than ever before, then the threat must be dire indeed.

Immortal 5 (Mahabali):

"In surrender, you will find your true strength. Do not fear the burden, Rishab. We have all borne it."

Mahabali, the once-great Asura king, spoke with a steady voice, his presence calm and grounded. His words were a reminder that even the greatest of kings had surrendered their power for the greater good. His immortality was granted not because of strength, but because of his willingness to surrender.

Rishab felt the weight of Mahabali's words settle on him like a mantle of responsibility. He had lived a life of solitude, but now he was being called to action.

Before he could respond, another figure stepped forward—**Parashurama**, the immortal warrior-sage, whose presence radiated a raw, primal energy. In his hands, he held the ancient **axe** that had felled kings and armies alike.

Immortal 6 (Parashurama):

"You are no longer just a seeker of moksha, Rishab. You must now become the protector of time itself. The weight of this battle will test your soul, but you are not alone. We will stand with you."

Parashurama's words were firm, resolute. The task before Rishab was not just a spiritual one; it was a battle, a war against forces that sought to tear the fabric of reality apart.

The final figure to step forward was **Kripacharya**, the wise teacher of the Kurus, his form radiating a quiet, contemplative energy. His presence was calming, like the still waters of a deep lake.

Immortal 7 (Kripacharya):

"Your time of peace has ended, Rishab. You are now a guardian of existence itself. There is no turning back."

Kripacharya's words were gentle but carried an undeniable truth. Rishab's path had shifted irrevocably. The life of isolation and peace he had known was over. He was no longer merely a seeker of moksha—he had become a **guardian of time**, responsible for the balance of all existence.

As Rishab stood before the Seven Immortals, their divine presence filling the space around him, he felt the crushing weight of his destiny settle on his shoulders. He had spent his life preparing to transcend the material world, to escape the cycle of rebirth. And now, the very thing he had sought to escape had become his responsibility to protect.

The Immortals could sense Rishab's hereettion. Another stepped forward, holding out a glowing object—a **small, metallic chip**, pulsing with energy far beyond anything Rishab had ever seen. It seemed to hum with both **mystical power and futuristic technology**, a fusion of worlds.

Without a word, the Immortal pressed the chip into Rishab's chest. A sudden, intense surge of energy shot through Rishab's body, filling him with **immense power**. His muscles tensed, his mind expanded, and his senses exploded with heightened awareness. He could feel the power settling within him—strength, speed, resilience, and the ability to manipulate time itself.

But there was a catch. **The powers would only awaken when his mind was still**. His body would move and fight, but his mind would have to remain calm, detached from the physical world. It was a paradox—a warrior who could only act when his mind was at peace.

Parashurama (Immortal 6):

"Your powers will only awaken when your mind is still. Your body will act, but your mind must meditate."

Rishab looked down at the chip now fused with his being, his mind racing. He had never sought power—he had only sought peace. And yet, the Immortals had granted him abilities far beyond the reach of ordinary men. The **burden of stopping Moksha**, of saving the future, now rested squarely on his shoulders.

Rishab (in thought):

I have never sought power. And yet...

He looked up at the Seven Immortals, their divine forms still radiating immense power. They had chosen him, and now, there was no turning back.

Vyasa (Immortal 3):

"You have always been connected to Moksha, Rishab. In every life, you have faced him, and each time the battle has grown more dangerous. But this time, you have the power to end it."

Rishab felt the weight of their words sink in, the enormity of his destiny becoming clear. He had never wanted this. His life had been one of **spiritual pursuit**, of seeking moksha and transcending the mortal plane. But now, he was being called to **fight**—not just for his own liberation, but for the **salvation of time itself**.

Ashwatthama (Immortal 1):

"The balance of time is in your hands, Rishab. The future depends on your actions."

Rishab bowed his head, the reality of his situation crashing over him like a tidal wave. His journey was no longer just about finding inner peace. It was about saving the very fabric of time and existence from unraveling.

Chapter 3

The Quantum Yogi

Rishab felt the familiar pull of time ripple through his mind, the sensation no longer foreign but still disorienting. The chip implanted in his chest pulsed, carrying him beyond the present, unraveling the fabric of his consciousness and thrusting him into the vast tapestry of his past lives. **This was no ordinary meditation**—this was time itself bending, showing him the **lives he had lived before**.

Each time he traveled back, it was as if a door had opened into another era, another existence, where his soul had fought the same battle against **Moksha**, the ancient enemy. But this time, something was different. The memories came faster, harder, the intensity of the past pressing on him more fiercely than ever before.

Suddenly, Rishab was no longer in the **Immortal Realm**. He stood on a vast, sprawling battlefield, the **air thick with smoke and the stench of war**. The **clash of steel** echoed around him, soldiers screaming as they fought in the distance. His hands gripped the hilt of a **massive sword**, his muscles tensed, ready for combat. He recognized this place—it was centuries ago, in an ancient war where he had once fought as a warrior, defending his kingdom. This was not the first time he had encountered **Moksha**.

Rishab (in thought):

This is familiar. I have fought here before. But when?

His eyes scanned the battlefield, and then he saw him—**Moksha**. In this incarnation, **Moksha** was a **fierce warlord**, clad in dark, imposing armor, his eyes glowing with malevolent intensity. He radiated power, his presence commanding the battlefield. Yet, despite the danger and the carnage surrounding them, **Rishab felt no fear**. He had faced **Moksha** before, in this life and in others. Each time, he had stood victorious, no matter the form Moksha had taken.

Rishab (in thought):

I have faced you before, Moksha, and I will defeat you again.

With a roar, Rishab charged across the battlefield, his sword raised high. His weapon clashed with **Moksha's**, the force of the impact sending tremors through the earth. The two men battled fiercely, their movements precise, each strike calculated. **Rishab fought with the skill and determination of a seasoned warrior**, his body remembering the art of war from this past life. The battle seemed endless, their swords clanging as time itself seemed to slow around them. But in the end, **Rishab struck a decisive blow**. **Moksha fell to the ground**, defeated.

As Rishab stood victorious, a strange feeling crept over him. **The battlefield began to fade**, the smoke dissipating, the sounds of war quieting to nothing. He had won, just as he had done before. **Moksha lay dead at his feet**.

But why did it feel incomplete?

The battlefield evaporated like a dream, and suddenly, the familiar **tug of time seized him once again**.

Now, **Rishab found himself in the quiet halls of an ancient library**. Rows of scrolls and books surrounded him. He was no longer a warrior but a scholar, dressed in simple robes, his hands ink-stained from years of study. In this life, he had fought **Moksha** not with weapons, but with intellect. He remembered the **games of strategy**, the **battles of the mind**, where he had uncovered **Moksha's plans** to manipulate history and had stopped him using logic and knowledge.

Rishab (in thought):

I stopped him here too, not with a sword, but with wisdom.

Across the table from him sat a version of **Moksha**, this time a **cunning politician**, his words sharp as knives. **Rishab could see the malice in Moksha's eyes** as they debated the future of an empire, each argument a move in a complex chess game. **Rishab's mind worked quickly**, countering **Moksha's every attempt** to twist the course of history. And just like in the battlefields of old, **he emerged victorious**, outmaneuvering Moksha at every turn, outthinking him at every twist and trap.

Once again, **Moksha fell**, defeated by knowledge instead of brute force. **Rishab's victory felt assured**.

Rishab (to himself):

No matter the form, Moksha, you cannot win.

But before he could revel in the victory, the scene faded, and **Rishab was pulled through time once again**.

This time, **he was standing atop a mountain**—a great temple behind him, a storm brewing on the horizon. **Moksha**, in this incarnation, was a **sorcerer**, commanding the elements, his power drawn from the darkest of magics. Lightning cracked the sky as they stood, staring each other down.

Rishab (in thought):

Magic cannot save you, Moksha.

They fought with spells and ancient incantations, **Moksha weaving dark spells of destruction**, while **Rishab countered with the magic of light and protection**. The air around them crackled with energy as they clashed. But, as in every incarnation before, **Rishab emerged victorious**, **defeating Moksha's dark magic with his light**.

Rishab (in thought):

I have defeated you in every lifetime. Why should this be any different?

Time folded again, and Rishab found himself on another battlefield, this time in a **desert**. In this life, **he was an**

archer, his body draped in golden armor. **Moksha**, now a general of an immense army, stood at the forefront. His chariot rode toward Rishab, the wind whipping the sand into a frenzy. **Rishab's bow twanged**, and his arrows flew true, each one striking down soldiers, each one weakening Moksha's forces. And then the final arrow, infused with the divine power of the gods, pierced **Moksha's heart**.

Each scene that played before him was another **victory**, another **defeat for Moksha**. **Rishab had stood against Moksha in many forms**, in many ages, sometimes as a king, other times as a wanderer or a holy man. In each life, **Moksha took on a new shape**: a **king, a sorcerer, a warrior, a politician**, but always driven by the same **relentless ambition**, the same desire to control **time, power, and destiny**.

Each time, **Rishab** stood as the force that would bring him down. **Every life was a testament** to Rishab's skill, his strength, his resilience. His victories, played out over the course of **centuries**, felt like a grand tapestry, one that had been woven together by the hands of the universe itself.

He had won in **nine lives**, **each time defeating Moksha**, each time emerging as the hero. But something about these victories left him uneasy.

Rishab (in thought):

I have bested you in every form, in every age. Why should this be any different?

The memories of his victories, his triumphs, **fed his growing confidence**. He had always stood stronger, smarter, more prepared than **Moksha**. If history had shown him anything, it was that he was **destined to triumph once again**. The thought filled him with **a sense of invincibility**, a certainty that **he could never lose**.

But **deep in the back of his mind**, the **Immortals' warning echoed**—a faint reminder of the danger ahead.

Immortal's Warning (echoing in Rishab's thoughts):

"This time will be different. Moksha's power has grown. He is not the same enemy you faced before."

Rishab shook off the thought. It didn't matter. He had always been **stronger, smarter**, more prepared than Moksha. **If history had shown him anything**, it was that **he could—and would—win again**. His **overconfidence swelled**, blocking out the creeping sense of doubt that threatened to rise.

Then came the dreams.

For weeks after these **time jumps**, Rishab found himself plagued by visions—**dreams of Moksha's death**. But these dreams were different. In them, it wasn't Rishab who struck the final blow. Instead, a shadowy figure loomed, a presence both familiar and unknown, striking down Moksha with a force that shook the heavens.

Rishab awoke from these dreams, **sweating and disoriented**. Each time, he was convinced it was his **past self** killing Moksha, that it was **he who had ended Moksha's life**, not this mysterious figure. The dreams confused him, blending his memories of victory with the unsettling image of someone else bringing Moksha's end.

Rishab (in thought):

It must have been me. I have defeated him in every lifetime.

But as the dreams continued, they became harder to dismiss. Each time, the figure became clearer, more defined, and the sense that **it wasn't him** became stronger.

Outside of his dreams, **Rishab's daily life continued**. He still awoke before dawn, practicing **his asanas and breathwork**, but something in him had changed. **The power granted to him by the Immortals** hummed in his body like a dormant storm, only awakening in times of need. At times, he felt a rush of energy so powerful that it took all his discipline to maintain control. On other days, he found himself using the powers to help in **mundane tasks**—making chores easier, bending time to complete work faster, even **pausing time momentarily** just to enjoy the peace of a still morning.

But there was a subtle danger in these powers. **Rishab's laziness began to creep in**. He found himself occasionally using his powers not for good, but for convenience. **Tasks that once required discipline now seemed trivial**. He could **bend time** to his will, avoid work, and indulge in leisure. And while he occasionally used his powers to **help those around him**, he knew deep down that this was not the purpose the Immortals had granted them for.

Still, **his confidence grew**. His daily life seemed manageable, even easy, with the powers. He began to believe that his destiny to defeat **Moksha** would unfold just as easily.

His **past identities** swirled in his mind, each life blending into the next. The memories of his **past victories** were clear, but as they merged within his body, they created a **complex web of egos**. At times, he felt like the **warrior king** with unmatched skill on the battlefield; at other times, he felt like the **scholar**, confident in his knowledge and strategy. Each identity fed into his **growing overconfidence**, a sense that no matter which life he drew from, **he was always superior to Moksha**.

But within him, there was also **chaos**. The merging of his past selves left him conflicted, at times unsure of who he truly was. Was he the peaceful seeker of moksha? Was he the warrior? Was he the scholar, the sage, the archer, the king? **All of these identities vied for control** within him, and though he often felt powerful, there were moments of doubt, moments when he questioned if he could truly balance all the lives he had lived.

The more he drew from his past victories, the more the line between **self-confidence and arrogance** blurred. **The Immortals' warning** echoed faintly in the back of his mind, but he dismissed it, believing that his **past triumphs would always carry him forward**. Each victory in his past had reinforced the belief that **he was destined to win again**.

But **deep down**, the sense of **unease** lingered, like a shadow that grew with each passing day. Rishab had seen

Moksha's machine, powered by **immortal blood**, blending **science and magic** in ways that defied logic. He had glimpsed the **destruction Moksha could unleash**, and yet, his confidence overpowered his fear.

Moksha had been defeated before, time and time again. And Rishab was certain, beyond any doubt, that **this time would be no different**.

Rishab (to himself):

I have defeated him in every era. Why should this one be any different?

But **something tugged at the edge of his thoughts**—the **Immortals' warning**, the **subtle sense of unease**. In the silence of his meditation, he could hear their words echoing, reminding him that **this time was not like the others**. But Rishab's overconfidence swelled, a force so strong that it drowned out the warning.

As Rishab stood on the cusp of battle, his **past lives**, his **memories**, and his **arrogance** merged into one. He was ready to face **Moksha** once again—but this time, **he might not be as prepared as he thought**.

Chapter 4

The Burden of Being Chosen

Rishab's eyes fluttered open as the early morning sun pierced through the gaps in the wooden shutters of his small cottage. The golden rays cast long, slanted shadows across the room, highlighting the simple furnishings—a wooden table, a clay water jug, and a few cooking utensils. Outside, the village began to stir. The crisp air carried the distant sounds of cattle being herded and the occasional chatter of villagers greeting the day. Rishab lay still for a moment, feeling the coolness of the morning breeze brush across his face.

The village beyond his doorstep was peaceful, unhurried—an illusion of simplicity and calm. The thatched rooftops of houses, the muddy paths winding through the village, and the routine of daily chores all painted a picture of a world untouched by the chaos he knew was coming. But for Rishab, this tranquility was a fleeting mirage, a pause in the grander scheme of cosmic turmoil. The weight of memories from his past lives pressed on his mind, lingering like shadows he could never shake off. He had witnessed centuries of wars, suffered the rise and fall of empires, and now, in this quiet corner of the world, he existed in a state of detachment.

Slowly, he rose from his mat, his movements deliberate, as though each action was a reflection of a memory he had already lived. His body hummed with immense power beneath the surface—power that was both a gift and a burden. He moved through his morning routine mechanically, each task so mundane and trivial compared to the knowledge and responsibility he now carried. Fetching water, sweeping the floor, preparing breakfast—each chore was done with precision but without thought.

As he moved, the memories of his past lives flickered in his mind, merging and swirling like an overwhelming tide. Sometimes he felt the strength of the warrior king, other times the wisdom of the scholar or the strategic brilliance of the general. His body was one, but within him were thousands of years of lives lived, experiences that made him something far greater—and far more distant—from the villagers who surrounded him.

Rishab (in thought):

These villagers... their lives are so small compared to the burden I carry. How can they understand?

As Rishab prepared his morning meal, he noticed a clay pot perched precariously on the edge of the counter. Before he could react, the pot slipped, shattering on the floor with a loud crash.

But Rishab didn't flinch. He stood still for a moment, his eyes closing, and in a practiced motion, he reached deep into himself, feeling the flow of time bend around him. It was as natural to him as breathing. The chip embedded in his chest pulsed, and the world around him responded.

Time rewound itself, the pieces of the clay pot flying back together, reforming until it was whole again, perfectly balanced on the counter as if nothing had ever happened.

Rishab (to himself):

Time bends to my will. What is there to worry about?

This had become his new normal. The use of his powers—once something he had been cautious with, reverent even—was now second nature. Every mistake, every inconvenience, was reversed with ease. If he missed a step while sweeping the floor, he simply rewound time and corrected it. If he spilled water from the jug, he moved back a few seconds and fixed the error. It had begun with small things—an act of convenience, perhaps even amusement. But now, Rishab found himself relying on his powers more and more.

No task was too small for him to manipulate time. He no longer felt the need to struggle with the day-to-day imperfections of life. If something broke, he fixed it. If he grew tired or careless, he rewound time and tried again. And while he knew in the depths of his mind that such trivial uses of his powers were beneath him, it was easier than facing the real challenges that loomed on the horizon.

Outside the cottage, the village continued with its daily routine. Rishab could hear the rhythmic thud of farmers working in the fields, the clatter of tools being repaired, and the faint sounds of children laughing as they played by the river. These villagers—people he had lived among for so long—now felt like strangers. Their concerns, their lives, their struggles were nothing compared to the weight he carried. Time, for them, was something linear, moving forward without pause. For Rishab, time was a tool, a force that bent and shifted at his command.

He wandered outside, his eyes distant and unfocused as he walked through the village. The villagers greeted him with respect and admiration, as they always had. He had lived among them for years, helping them with their crops, fixing broken tools, and offering advice when needed. But now, Rishab barely acknowledged them. His mind was elsewhere, in the future—in the battle that was to come.

The villagers did not know of his true nature. To them, he was simply Rishab—the humble sage who lived on the edge of the village. But to Rishab, he was something far more. He was no longer one of them. The simple concerns of their lives—the harvest, the weather, the fixing of tools—were beneath him.

Rishab (in thought):

What do they know of the true danger that awaits? They worry about their crops while the fabric of time itself unravels.

As he passed the fields, a group of farmers struggled to lift a large boulder blocking their irrigation channel. They had been trying all morning, and their frustration was palpable. One of them saw Rishab approaching and waved him over.

Farmer (with a respectful tone):

"Rishab-ji, can you help us move this stone? We've tried, but it's too heavy."

Rishab paused, looking down at the stone. He could move it with a mere flick of his wrist. His strength, one of the gifts granted by the Immortals, was limitless. The stone was no more an obstacle to him than a pebble. But as he stood there, staring at the boulder and the struggling villagers, a sense of detachment washed over him.

He no longer saw the significance in such tasks. Why bother? What was a stone compared to the cosmic battle that loomed ahead? Moksha, the destroyer of worlds, was coming. The future of time itself was at risk. And here were these villagers, worried about a stone blocking their field.

Rishab sighed internally. What did it matter?

With a single motion, he lifted the stone and tossed it aside as if it weighed nothing. The farmers thanked him profusely, their gratitude overflowing. But Rishab barely heard their words. He turned away, already lost in his own thoughts. He could help them with their mundane struggles, but it meant nothing to him. His mind was on greater things—on the battle with Moksha, on the future that hung in the balance.

Rishab (in thought):

These people... they don't understand. They never will.

As the day wore on, Rishab wandered through the village, helping where he could, though his detachment was palpable. He no longer felt connected to the villagers or their simple way of life. His powers had set him apart, elevating him above the everyday struggles of those around him.

In the evening, as the sun set behind the hills, Rishab stood at the edge of the village, staring out at the distant horizon. The air was cool, the sky painted in shades of orange and pink, and yet, Rishab felt nothing.

Suddenly, a young boy from the village approached. The boy had been struggling all day with a broken plow, unable to fix it despite his best efforts. He looked up at Rishab with wide, hopeful eyes, holding the broken plow in his hands.

Boy (nervously):

"Rishab-ji, could you help me fix the plow? The field is ready, but I can't get it working."

Rishab glanced down at the boy, his expression blank. In an instant, he saw the boy's entire life unfold before him—his struggles, his future, his eventual death. It all seemed so insignificant. What did a broken plow matter in the face of eternity? Rishab could fix it with a mere thought. He could reverse time to the moment before the plow broke. But what was the point?

Rishab (in thought):

What does it matter? What is a broken plow compared to the collapse of time itself?

He looked away, his gaze drifting to the horizon once more. In his mind, the Immortals' words echoed, reminding him of the battle ahead, the danger Moksha posed. What was this plow, this boy, this village, compared to that?

And yet, as he turned to walk away, something inside him stirred. It was faint, barely a whisper beneath the overwhelming tide of his arrogance. But it was there—a voice he had long since buried. Was he losing his connection to the world he was meant to protect?

The boy stood there, his eyes wide with expectation, waiting for Rishab to do something. This small, insignificant moment was the boy's entire world.

Rishab sighed, pushing aside the conflicting emotions. With a wave of his hand, the plow was fixed, the metal glowing briefly as it restored itself. The boy's face lit up with joy, and he thanked Rishab profusely before running off to the fields.

Rishab (in thought):

These people... they don't understand. They never will.

As the sun dipped below the horizon, casting the world in shadow, Rishab returned to his small cottage. Inside, the air was still. The only sound was the soft creak of the wooden floor as he sat cross-legged on the ground. He closed his eyes and tried to meditate, to return to the peace he had once sought with such fervor.

But it was futile. The memories of his past lives pressed in on him, unrelenting. The battles, the victories, the warnings from the Immortals—they all swirled in his mind like a storm, refusing to quiet. And always, in the distance, he felt the looming presence of Moksha, like a shadow over time itself.

Rishab (in thought):

I was never meant for this. I sought moksha, not this endless burden of power and destiny.

But that was no longer his path. Moksha was a distant dream, eclipsed by the cosmic battle he had been drawn into. His journey was no longer about personal enlightenment or peace. It was about power, destiny, and the responsibility of guarding time itself. And the more powerful he became, the more isolated he felt.

The world around him—the village, the people, the simple concerns of daily life—had become small, insignificant. And yet, in the quiet moments when he allowed himself to reflect, Rishab feared that he was losing himself in the process.

Chapter 5

The Sword and the Sheild

The sun had barely risen over the horizon when Rishab felt it—a disturbance in the stillness of the jungle that had been his sanctuary for so long. The serenity that typically greeted him in the early hours of the morning was abruptly pierced by a sharp, unnatural shift in the air. Rishab, seated cross-legged in meditation near his cottage, slowly opened his eyes. The hum of nature around him—the rustle of leaves, the chirping of birds—had grown muted, as if the jungle itself had fallen into an uneasy silence.

His heightened awareness immediately picked up on the presence of others moving swiftly through the forest. Their movements were deliberate, hurried, and full of purpose. Rishab could feel it, a subtle vibration through the ground, a ripple in the calm he had so carefully cultivated. He stood up, his body alert, his senses expanding to take in the energy of the forest.

Rishab (in thought):

Something's coming. Something dangerous.

For weeks, Rishab had contented himself with the quiet solitude of the jungle, distancing himself from the concerns of the outside world. He had spent this time reflecting on the immense power that flowed through him, on the past lives that haunted his thoughts, and on the battle that was to come with Moksha. Yet, despite his efforts to remain detached, the world beyond his sanctuary was pressing in. **The future was encroaching upon the present**, and Rishab could no longer ignore it.

He heard it then—**the unmistakable clang of steel against steel**—followed by the grunts and shouts of combat. His body moved before his mind could fully process the situation. With an instinct born from centuries of battle, Rishab darted into the dense underbrush, his steps swift and silent. **The forest blurred around him** as he ran, his speed far beyond that of a normal man. The jungle, once his place of peace and reflection, had transformed into a battleground.

As he neared the source of the commotion, he felt the **pulsing energy** of something ancient, something powerful. It was a relic of unimaginable strength, something that should have remained hidden. **Moksha's men**—it had to be them.

When he reached the edge of a clearing, the sight that greeted him was chaotic and intense. **Two figures**—young, strong, and determined—fought against a group of men clad in dark, tactical armor. Their movements were sharp and precise, a seamless blend of training and instinct.

The first was **Roshan**, a tall and powerful figure, his muscles rippling beneath his simple tunic as he wielded a staff with **deadly precision**. Each movement was calculated, and his eyes burned with a **fierce intensity** as he fought off the attackers. His strikes were swift, his body moving with the grace of a trained warrior, and yet, there was a **protective desperation** in his stance.

Beside him was **Reet**, her lithe form moving with an **elegant ferocity**. She dodged and weaved through the chaos of the fight, her sharp intellect evident in every calculated strike. She moved like a dancer, anticipating the attackers' movements before they even made them. Her eyes, fierce and determined, scanned the battlefield for any weakness in the enemy's defense. **Rishab was captivated by her presence**, an instant and deep connection stirring within him—something beyond admiration, something primal and ancient. His heart, burdened with centuries of isolation, was moved in an instant. **Reet's grace, her strength, her intellect—it all spoke to him in a way that no one else had in lifetimes.**

Together, **Roshan and Reet** fought as a seamless unit, their movements synchronized as if they had been fighting side by side their entire lives. But despite their skill, **they were outnumbered**. The men in the tactical armor moved with ruthless efficiency, clearly intent on retrieving the ancient weapon that one of them clutched tightly in his hand—a weapon that glowed faintly with a light that seemed to pulse in time with the heartbeat of the earth.

Rishab (in thought):

Moksha's men... they're after the weapon. This is worse than I thought.

Roshan's staff whirled through the air, the wood cracking against the armor of an assailant, sending him sprawling to the ground. But as Roshan turned to parry another blow, one of the attackers **broke through their defenses**. His weapon raised, the assailant charged toward Reet, who had been momentarily distracted while fending off two others. **Time seemed to slow** for Rishab as he watched the attacker close in on her, his weapon poised to strike.

Rishab (in thought):

No!

Without thinking, **Rishab moved**. His body became a blur of speed as he darted across the clearing. In the blink of an eye, he was at Reet's side. The attacker's weapon swung downward, but before it could land, **Rishab caught the man's arm mid-swing**. The force of Rishab's grip sent the assailant flying backward with inhuman strength, crashing through the trees with a thud.

Reet spun around, her eyes wide with shock as she realized that her life had been saved by a stranger. **Their eyes met for a brief moment**, and in that instant, something passed between them—an unspoken connection, a recognition of something deeper than the circumstances at hand.

But there was no time for gratitude. The remaining attackers, sensing their opportunity, **vanished into the forest**, retreating with the stolen weapon in hand. **The relic was gone**.

Roshan, seeing the escape, **whirled around**, his eyes blazing with fury and suspicion. His protective instinct for Reet, combined with the failure to retrieve the weapon, ignited a fire within him.

Roshan (furiously):

"You're with them, aren't you? I won't let you take Reet!"

Without waiting for a response, **Roshan charged at Rishab**, his staff raised and ready to strike. His movements were fueled by a **mix of rage and fear**, and his blows were fast and relentless. Rishab barely had time to react, his body still adjusting to the surge of adrenaline that had come with saving Reet. **Roshan's strikes were powerful and precise**, his staff spinning through the air in deadly arcs.

Rishab blocked the first few blows, his reflexes honed by centuries of battle, but he could see the fire in Roshan's eyes—**a fire fueled by suspicion, fear, and frustration**. Roshan wasn't going to stop until he had answers.

Rishab:

"Wait, I'm not your enemy!"

Roshan's eyes narrowed, his staff spinning for another strike.

Roshan (furiously):

"Then why did you let them get away? You're working with them, aren't you?"

Rishab took a step back, **avoiding the next strike**. He could see the raw emotion in Roshan's face—the fear of losing Reet, the frustration of failing to retrieve the weapon, and the deep-seated suspicion that Rishab was somehow involved with the attackers.

But beyond the surface, Rishab could also see **something else**: **Roshan's fierce loyalty to Reet**, a loyalty that was driving him to protect her at all costs. To Roshan, Rishab was just another threat, another unknown variable in an already dangerous situation.

Rishab:

"I'm not with them! I was trying to help!"

Before Roshan could respond, **Reet stepped forward**, her hand reaching out to touch her brother's shoulder. Her gaze remained locked on Rishab, her eyes scanning him as if trying to piece together the puzzle of who he was.

Reet:

"Wait! He saved me. He's not our enemy, Roshan."

Roshan hereetted, the tension in his body **slowly easing** as Reet's words sank in. His grip on his staff remained tight, but he lowered it slightly, his eyes still full of **wary suspicion** as they lingered on Rishab.

For a moment, the three of them stood in silence, the clearing still and quiet. The only sound was the rustling of the wind through the trees and the distant call of birds in the jungle. **Reet's gaze never left Rishab**, her mind clearly racing as she processed what had just happened.

Reet (cautiously):

"Who are you?"

Rishab took a deep breath, knowing that the time had come to reveal more than he had wanted. He had lived in isolation for so long, believing that his mission was a solitary one. But now, it was becoming increasingly clear that he would need **allies**—whether he liked it or not.

Rishab:

"My name is Rishab. I've been chosen by the Immortals to stop Moksha. I'm not here to harm you—I'm here to stop him."

Roshan's grip tightened on his staff again, the words striking him like a blow. He had heard enough **myths and legends** in his life to recognize when something was beyond the realm of ordinary, but this? The Immortals? A man chosen to stop Moksha? It all sounded **impossible**. Yet, there was something about Rishab—something in his voice, in the way he carried himself—that gave Roshan pause.

Reet, however, was quicker to grasp the gravity of what Rishab was saying. Her mind, always sharp and analytical, was already making connections. The **ancient weapon** they had been sent to retrieve, the growing strength of **Moksha's forces**, the legends of the seven

Immortals—and now, this man standing before them, claiming to be their chosen one.

Reet (with a calculated tone):

"If what you're saying is true, then why haven't we heard of you before? Why now?"

Rishab's expression darkened as memories of the visions flooded his mind—the warnings from the Immortals, the destruction he had witnessed in his mind's eye, the power that coursed through his veins.

Rishab:

"Because now is when Moksha's plan comes to fruition. He's been using technology from the future—something far more dangerous than anything you've seen. He's manipulating time itself, and unless we stop him, the present will be destroyed."

Roshan and Reet exchanged a glance, the weight of Rishab's words settling heavily between them. **Roshan's distrust still simmered**, but there was a growing understanding in his eyes. **Reet's brow furrowed** as she considered the enormity of what Rishab was saying. The pieces of the puzzle were falling into place, but they revealed a **picture far more terrifying** than either of them had anticipated.

Roshan (coldly):

"And we're just supposed to believe you?

You show up out of nowhere, and suddenly you're here to save the world?"

Rishab's patience was wearing thin. He understood Roshan's suspicion, but there was no time for doubt. **The stakes were too high**, and the enemy was already moving. Rishab had spent centuries preparing for this moment, and the time for hereettion had long passed.

Rishab (firmly):

"You don't have to believe me. But whether you like it or not, we're on the same side. We're fighting the same enemy."

A long silence fell over the clearing as the tension between the three hung in the air. The jungle around them seemed to hold its breath, waiting for what would happen next.

Finally, it was **Reet** who broke the silence, her voice calm but full of urgency.

Reet:

"Roshan, he saved me. And if he's telling the truth... we can't afford to turn him away."

Roshan exhaled sharply, the frustration still evident in his eyes, but the tension in his body finally eased. He lowered his staff completely, though his gaze remained fixed on Rishab with **a mixture of suspicion and grudging respect**.

Roshan (reluctantly):

"We'll see. But if you're lying, or if you're working for Moksha, I will kill you..."

Rishab met his gaze, unwavering.

Rishab (with quiet resolve):

"I'm not."

The moment passed, and with it, the urgency of their situation returned. **The attackers had escaped with the weapon**, and time was running out. Whether they trusted each other or not, Rishab, Roshan, and Reet would have to work together if they were going to stop **Moksha's plans**.

The jungle around them seemed to stir once more, the wind picking up as if the world itself was aware of the impending storm. As the three stood together, a fragile alliance formed—one built on **necessity**, but one that would soon be tested in ways they could not yet imagine.

Chapter 6

Warriors of Humanity

The journey to the **Chirayu Foundation's base** was long and filled with tension, an uneasy silence settling between the trio as they moved through the dense, ancient forest. The towering trees, their canopies stretching high above, filtered the sunlight into soft, dappled patterns on the jungle floor. **Roshan** led the way, his body moving with the precision and alertness of a seasoned warrior. He sliced through the undergrowth with his blade, cutting a swift path through the dense vegetation. **Reet** followed closely behind, her steps measured and deliberate, though her gaze occasionally flicked back to **Rishab**, who trailed slightly behind.

Rishab kept his distance, his mind racing with the events that had unfolded over the past few hours. The weight of the encounter with **Moksha's forces** still pressed heavily on him, along with the sudden turn of events that had brought him into the company of these two warriors. Despite the calm that usually defined his demeanor, Rishab couldn't shake the growing sense of unease. **Roshan's distrust** was palpable—his silence as sharp as his blade—and Rishab could sense that the path ahead would not be easy.

Rishab (in thought):

There's no escaping this now. I must earn their trust, but how?

The trio continued through the forest, the dense jungle giving way to more familiar trails as they moved closer to the foundation. The air grew cooler, the thick foliage becoming sparser, revealing glimpses of ancient structures hidden among the trees. **Rishab's heightened awareness** tingled, and he could sense the presence of powerful, unseen forces in the air, mingling with the remnants of ancient magic. As they trekked deeper, the environment around them felt charged, as if **the very ground they walked on hummed with energy**—a sacredness that was hard to define, yet impossible to ignore.

Rishab (in thought):

This place... it's older than I imagined. They've been preparing for this for centuries.

For hours, they marched in near silence, the occasional snap of twigs or rustle of leaves the only sounds interrupting the quiet. **Reet** occasionally glanced back at Rishab, her expression unreadable, but her eyes sharp, calculating. Though she had shown a willingness to believe Rishab's story, her guard was still up, and Rishab could sense her mind working, piecing together everything that had transpired. **Roshan**, on the other hand, had not spoken a word since their encounter with **Moksha's men**. His mistrust hung in the air, unspoken but ever-present.

As they approached their destination, Rishab noticed the **first signs of the Chirayu Foundation's base**. The air grew heavier with a sense of ancient purpose, and through the trees, he could make out the towering walls of an imposing structure. Hidden deep within the jungle, the base was an architectural marvel that blended seamlessly with the natural landscape. The outer walls were high and formidable, made of dark stone etched with ancient symbols that glowed faintly in the dimming light. At first glance, the structure appeared to be a temple, its exterior worn with the passage of time, but there was something more to it—something **far more modern** lurking beneath the surface.

As they passed through the outer gates, Rishab's suspicions were confirmed. The **Chirayu Foundation** had embraced both **the ancient and the modern**, blending the mystical and the technological into one. Inside the base, relics from battles long past were displayed alongside **advanced technology**—holographic displays, surveillance systems, and weaponry that looked as though it had been plucked from the distant future. It was a fortress of knowledge, designed to **safeguard powerful artifacts** and ensure that the magic of the past did not fall into the wrong hands.

Rishab (in thought):

This is more than a sanctuary. It's a stronghold. They've been fighting this war far longer than I realized.

Roshan and Reet led Rishab deeper into the compound, passing towering statues of gods and warriors, relics of ancient weapons, and glowing crystals that pulsed with unseen energy. **The atmosphere was thick with history**, the air heavy with the weight of centuries of knowledge and preparation. Rishab felt a strange sense of familiarity wash over him—this place, with its melding of myth and modernity, felt like the crossroads of everything he had been fighting for across lifetimes. Yet, there was a **tension** in the air, a tension that emanated not just from the place itself, but from the people within it.

As they neared a large, ornately carved door that led into the central chamber, Rishab could feel the **presence of power** behind it. The door creaked open slowly, revealing a **vast hall** lined with ancient murals and symbols. At the centre of the hall stood **Indra**, the leader of the Chirayu Foundation.

Indra was an imposing figure, his tall frishabe radiating authority and control. His **long silver hair** flowed over his shoulders, giving him an almost ethereal appearance, and his sharp, piercing eyes immediately locked onto Rishab. Unlike the warriors and scientists scattered throughout the compound, **Indra** carried an air of mysticism, his robes adorned with intricate symbols that spoke of ancient knowledge. He stood still, observing Rishab with a calm intensity, but Rishab could sense the **suspicion** beneath his calm exterior.

Roshan and Reet bowed slightly as they approached, a sign of respect for their leader. Rishab followed suit, though his gaze remained level with Indra's, refusing to lower his eyes. This was not a place for timidity—**Indra's approval was essential**, but Rishab could already feel the weight of the **judgment** that awaited him.

Indra (coldly):

"So, this is the man claiming to be chosen by the Immortals. The one who has supposedly fought Moksha in past lives."

The skepticism in his voice was palpable, and his eyes narrowed as he studied Rishab, as if examining a dangerous artifact that might explode at any moment. The hall was silent, the air thick with tension. **Rishab could feel the gaze of the others in the room**—the warriors, scholars, and engineers of the foundation—all watching, waiting to see how he would respond.

Rishab:

"I don't claim anything, Indra. I've been chosen by the Immortals to stop Moksha. It's not something I asked for, but it's my responsibility."

Indra remained still, his arms crossed, his gaze unflinching. His eyes glinted with a mixture of **curiosity and mistrust**, as though he were weighing Rishab's words against his own internal calculations. He seemed unimpressed by Rishab's statement, though there was a hint of something deeper—a flicker of recognition at the gravity of what was being discussed.

Indra:

"Responsibility? You speak of responsibility as if you understand the burden it carries. Do you have any idea what we have sacrificed to keep the world safe from those who would misuse its power?"

Indra gestured toward the relics lining the walls—**ancient weapons**, scrolls filled with **forbidden knowledge**, artifacts capable of untold destruction. **Rishab could feel the energy radiating from them**, each relic a reminder of the ancient forces at play. The **Chirayu Foundation** had clearly been fighting this war for centuries, and it was clear that they had no reason to trust someone who claimed to be "chosen."

Indra (firmly):

"We've dealt with men like you before. Men who think they have the right to wield the power of the ancients. And every one of them has been a threat to everything we stand for."

Rishab's jaw clenched. He had expected **doubt**, but the intensity of Indra's words still stung. He knew that the foundation had fought countless battles to protect the world, but he was not here to steal their power or take control. **He was here to stop the same enemy they had been fighting**—the enemy that now threatened the very fabric of time.

Rishab:

"I understand your doubts, Indra. But I'm not here to take your power. I've fought Moksha across lifetimes. He's manipulating time itself, and if we don't stop him, the future will be destroyed."

The room fell silent. **Indra's eyes flickered with something**—perhaps recognition of the **gravity** of Rishab's words. Roshan and Reet exchanged glances, the tension between them clear, but there was a moment of pause, as though they too were considering the truth behind Rishab's warning.

Still, **Indra remained unmoved**, though his expression grew more thoughtful. His arms were crossed tightly, his brow furrowed as he scrutinized Rishab. Indra's presence radiated strength, but beneath it was the burden of centuries of vigilance—a burden he would not let go of easily.

Indra:

"You expect us to believe that you've fought Moksha in past lives? That time itself bends to your will?"

Indra's voice was calm, but there was an **edge of steel** in his words. Rishab met his gaze head-on, refusing to back down. He knew that his story sounded **impossible**, but he also knew that the stakes were too high for half-truths.

Rishab (firmly):

"Yes. And I'm not asking you to believe me blindly. But you know Moksha's power. You've seen what he's capable of. His henchmen are stealing ancient weapons for a reason, and it's not just to wreak havoc in the present. He's trying to change the past to control the future."

The room remained silent, the weight of Rishab's words pressing down on them. **Indra's face remained impassive**, but there was a flicker of doubt in his eyes—a sign that, despite his outward skepticism, he understood the gravity of the situation.

After what felt like an eternity, **Indra spoke again**, though his tone remained cautious.

Indra:

"Even if what you say is true, that doesn't mean we can trust you. You have powers—abilities that none of us fully understand. Powers that could easily be used against us."

The accusation hung in the air, heavy and cold. Rishab exhaled slowly, feeling the weight of his task pressing down on him. He had lived in **isolation** for so long, believing that his fight was a personal one. But now he realized that he needed more than just his own strength—he needed **allies**, even if they doubted him.

Rishab:

"I understand your hereettion, Indra. But I'm not your enemy. I've seen the future, and if we don't work together, Moksha will destroy everything. This isn't just about one battle—it's about the survival of time itself."

For a long moment, **Indra remained silent**, his gaze fixed on Rishab. He seemed to be calculating, weighing the risks and the potential consequences of trusting this man who had appeared out of nowhere with such grand claims. But finally, Indra's expression softened—though only slightly.

Indra (quietly, but firmly):

"The Chirayu Foundation has survived for centuries because we are careful. We don't take chances. But I'll allow you to stay—under ***supervision****."*

Rishab nodded. It wasn't trust, but it was a step forward. He could feel the **weight of Indra's authority** in the room, but also the burden of his own mission. He had no choice but to **prove himself**, not just to Indra, but to everyone here.

Rishab (quietly):

"I'll prove myself. You'll see."

Indra's eyes remained hard, but there was a flicker of something more behind them—a hint of understanding, or perhaps a recognition of the **danger they all faced**. The foundation was not built on trust—it was built on **vigilance** and **sacrifice**. But if there was even a chance that Rishab's warning about Moksha was true, they could not afford to dismiss him outright.

As the tension in the room began to ease, **Roshan's eyes remained fixed on Rishab**, his suspicion still evident. He, like Indra, was not convinced.

Roshan (muttering under his breath):

"We'll see if he's really who he says he is. Or if he's just another Rakshasa in disguise."

Indra (seriously):

"I agree. If Rishab has any Rakshasa blood in him, I will see to it that we neutralize him before he becomes a threat."

Rishab's fists clenched at the accusation, but he held back his anger. He knew they were on edge, and he understood the deep-seated mistrust. However, the idea that he could be aligned with **Moksha's kind** was not something he could allow to stand.

Rishab (calmly but resolutely):

"I am no Rakshasa. You will see soon enough. I fight for this world, for time itself. And I will prove to you that I am a man of honor and good."

The path ahead was not going to be simple. Rishab's **alliance with the Chirayu Foundation** had begun, but the battles that awaited them would test more than just their strength. They would test their trust, their resolve, and the very limits of what it meant to **fight for the future**.

Chapter 7

The Trial of the Chosen

The **training grounds of the Chirayu Foundation** seemed to pulsate with life, a place where **myth and modernity** coexisted in perfect harmony. The air was thick with tension as **Rishab stood at the edge of the arena**, his eyes scanning the vast space that would soon serve as the battleground for his trial by combat. Towering relics of ancient battles loomed overhead, their surfaces etched with the symbols of gods and warriors long past. The ground beneath his feet, scarred and worn from centuries of conflict, seemed to hum with the echoes of the warriors who had trained and fought there before him.

Across the arena, **Indra** stepped forward, his figure imposing and unyielding. In his hands, he held a **mythical staff**, an ancient weapon imbued with the power of the elements. The staff crackled faintly with energy, arcs of lightning dancing along its surface. Rishab could feel its power from where he stood, a tangible force that sent a shiver down his spine. This wasn't just a weapon—it was a symbol of Indra's command over the forces of nature, and a challenge to Rishab's claim of strength.

Indra's eyes locked onto Rishab's with cold intensity. The leader of the **Chirayu Foundation** had made no secret of his skepticism, and now, the time had come for Rishab to prove himself. But this trial was more than just a test of combat skills—it was a test of control, of **identity**, of whether Rishab was truly who he claimed to be.

Indra (coldly):

"You claim to be chosen by the Immortals, to have fought Moksha across lifetimes. But words are meaningless in this place. We fight with proof. Let's see what kind of man you truly are."

The challenge hung in the air like a blade suspended between them. With a swift motion, **Indra struck the ground** with his staff, and the arena came alive. **Symbols etched into the walls began to glow**, their light intensifying as the relics lining the arena pulsed with a dormant magic now awakened by Indra's command. The air around Rishab became thick with energy, charged with a power that seemed to seep into his very bones.

Rishab took a deep breath, trying to steady himself. **This wasn't just about fighting—this was about proving that he could control the immense power inside him.** For days, the visions of his past lives had haunted him, memories of his battles with **Moksha** bleeding into the present. The line between his past and present selves had blurred, and with each passing day, the weight of those memories had grown heavier.

As Indra raised his staff, Rishab felt the energy around him shift. **The arena blurred**, and for a brief moment, he wasn't standing in the Chirayu Foundation's training grounds—he was on a battlefield from long ago, surrounded by the faces of warriors who had died fighting alongside him. The sound of clashing steel and the roar of war filled his ears. **Moksha's laughter echoed in his mind**, mocking him, taunting him.

Rishab blinked, trying to focus. This was no time to lose control. **Indra wasn't Moksha**, but the memories were so vivid, so real. He could almost feel the weight of the sword in his hand from a lifetime long past.

Rishab (in thought):

I am not Moksha. I'm not a Rakshasa. I've come to stop him, not to become him. I have to prove that I can control this power.

The words echoed in his mind, a desperate reminder of who he was—**who he still was**. **Rishab was no Rakshasa**, but the fear lingered. The fear that, like Moksha, the power within him could consume him, twist him into something unrecognizable. He had fought across lifetimes to prevent Moksha from unleashing chaos upon the world, and now, in this body, in this life, he was determined not to let that same darkness take hold of him.

But the visions—**why were they so strong?**

As if in response to his turmoil, **Indra attacked**. The staff crackled with energy as it swung toward Rishab, and for a moment, Rishab's vision blurred again. Indra's face flickered, replaced by the snarling visage of **Moksha**, his eyes gleaming with malice. **Rishab dodged the blow**, but the confusion rattled him. His heartbeat thundered in his ears, and his hands trembled.

Rishab (in thought):

Why do I see Moksha? What is happening to me?

The ground beneath him seemed to shift, becoming the blood-soaked earth of a battlefield from centuries ago. **Indra's staff morphed into the weapons of Moksha**—dark, twisted tools of destruction that Rishab had seen wielded by his nemesis in countless lives. Indra's form became a shadow of Moksha's towering presence, and Rishab's mind spiraled into chaos. He could feel the pull of the past, the **weight of his past lives** pressing down on him, threatening to drown him.

Indra's attacks came faster, the staff crackling with energy that seemed to draw on the very elements themselves. Lightning arced from the weapon, fire flared at its tip, and the ground beneath Rishab's feet trembled as Indra's mastery of the elements was on full display. Rishab blocked the strikes as best he could, but with each clash of their weapons, the visions grew stronger. **Moksha's face**, Moksha's voice—**it was all around him**.

Rishab (in thought, panicking):

Why can't I see clearly? Indra is not Moksha—this is not him! But why does it feel like I'm fighting him again?

He tried to focus, tried to remember where he was, but the **past was too powerful**. The arena blurred once again, and Rishab found himself on a battlefield from ages past. The screams of soldiers, the clang of swords, the stench of death—**it was all so real**. In this vision, **Moksha stood before him**, laughing as he swung his dark blade. The laughter echoed in Rishab's mind, mingling with the voices of his past incarnations.

Indra's voice cut through the chaos, but Rishab couldn't hear the words. All he saw was Moksha, and all he felt was the desperate urge to strike, to end this once and for all.

Rishab's breathing became ragged as **the pressure inside him built**. His control was slipping, the line between **hero and villain**, between **Rishab and Moksha**, becoming dangerously thin. And then, in a moment of sheer panic, Rishab lashed out with a fist imbued with the divine strength granted to him by the Immortals. **His punch cut through the air**, aimed straight at Indra's chest.

Indra barely managed to block the strike, but the force of the blow sent him staggering backward. **The impact was devastating**. Indra's staff absorbed some of the force, but the sheer power behind Rishab's attack left a scorch mark on the ground where Indra stood. For a moment, **Indra's face twisted in shock**, and Rishab saw the flicker of vulnerability in his eyes.

Rishab's heart pounded as he realized what had just happened. **He had almost killed Indra**. His breath came in ragged gasps, and his vision swam as the weight of what he had done crashed over him. **This was not Moksha**, but he had almost struck a fatal blow to a man who was not his enemy. **What was happening to him?**

He felt the darkness inside him, the same darkness that had consumed **Moksha**, threatening to consume him as well. His hands shook uncontrollably, his fingers clenching and unclenching as he fought to regain control. **The voices of his past incarnations** screamed in his mind, urging him to finish the fight, to destroy the enemy before him.

But **Indra was not the enemy**. Rishab knew this. He had to stop, had to regain control, but the visions were too strong, too vivid. He could feel himself slipping, losing himself to the chaos.

And then, through the fog of his mind, **Reet's voice** rang out, clear and sharp, cutting through the madness.

Reet (shouting):

"Rishab! Remember who you are! You are not him!"

Her words hit him like a lightning strike, cutting through the haze and pulling him back to reality. The vision of **Moksha** dissolved in an instant, and in its place stood **Indra**, battered but alive, his eyes still filled with a mixture of wariness and suspicion. Rishab's fist, which had been poised to deliver a second blow, lowered slowly as the energy that had surged through him began to fade.

Rishab stumbled backward, his breathing shallow and labored. **Reet's words** echoed in his mind, grounding him, reminding him of who he was—**who he still was**. He was not Moksha. **He was not a Rakshasa**. The power inside him did not define him—it was his to control, not the other way around.

The arena was silent now, the air heavy with the weight of what had just transpired. **Indra**, though visibly injured, stood tall, watching Rishab with a mixture of caution and curiosity. **Roshan and Reet** remained on the sidelines, their faces filled with concern.

The trial by combat was over, but the tension between Rishab and Indra remained palpable.

Indra (grimly):

"You're strong, no doubt about that. But strength without control is a threat, not an asset."

Rishab lowered his gaze, still catching his breath. He knew that **Indra was right**. His power was immense, but his control was slipping. The memories of his past lives, the endless battles against Moksha, were beginning to consume him. **He had come so close** to losing himself in the fight. He couldn't afford to let that happen again.

Rishab (softly, with remorse):

"I... I'm sorry. I didn't mean to—"

Indra (interrupting, sternly):

"It's not enough to just be powerful, Rishab. You claim to be here to stop Moksha, but if you can't control your own mind, you'll be more dangerous than he is."

The words stung, but **they were true**. Rishab had felt the truth of them in the moment when he had almost struck **Indra down**. The line between himself and **Moksha** was thinner than he had realized, and that realization left a **bitter taste** in his mouth. **He was not Moksha**, but he had come dangerously close to becoming him.

Rishab (with determination):

"You're right. I lost control. But I won't let it happen again."

Indra studied him for a long moment, the tension between them still thick. Finally, with a slight nod, **Indra lowered his staff**, though his eyes remained hard.

Indra (warning):

"See that it doesn't. Because next time, I won't be as forgiving."

The trial by combat had ended, but **Rishab's journey toward earning Indra's trust** was far from over. He had proven his physical strength, but now he had to prove his control—**over his powers**, over his mind, and over the **ghosts of his past**. The battle against **Moksha** loomed ever closer, and Rishab knew that if he couldn't master himself, he would never be able to defeat the darkness that awaited him.

Chapter 8

The Architects of Destruction

The **command room** of the **Chirayu Foundation** was a stark departure from the mystical and ancient atmosphere that filled the rest of the base. Unlike the relic-filled halls outside, this room was bathed in the glow of modern technology—**screens covered the walls**, each one streaming live data, historical maps, and reports of **Moksha's movements**. The air was thick with tension, and the hum of advanced machinery provided a constant undercurrent to the sense of urgency that filled the space.

Rishab stood at the edge of the room, alongside **Roshan** and **Reet**. His eyes were fixed on the central screen, waiting for the briefing to begin. The tension from the trial by combat still hung in the air, and despite his victory, Rishab could sense **Indra's lingering distrust**. But now was not the time to dwell on the past. There were more immediate concerns—**Moksha's forces were on the move**, and time was running out.

Indra's voice cut through the low hum of the command room as he stepped forward, his expression grim and resolute. His **silver hair** seemed to glow in the light of the screens, but there was no softness in his gaze. He had already seen too much destruction, and the stakes had never been higher.

Indra:

"Moksha's henchmen have already begun their operations in our timeline. These are no ordinary foot soldiers—they are as dangerous as he is, and each of them plays a critical role in his plan to rewrite history."

The main screen flickered to life, revealing the **first image**—a figure dressed in sleek, futuristic armor. His face was obscured by a helmet, but the faint outline of a **half-demon mask** suggested something far more sinister. The armor gleamed under the light of unknown, otherworldly energy, and the man's posture exuded **confidence** and **deadly precision**.

Indra (pointing to the screen):

"This is the first: a time-traveler from Moksha's future. He was sent back to secure ancient weapons and relics that Moksha needs to power his machine. We've tracked his movements across several key historical sites—each one tied to artifacts of immense power."

Rishab's eyes narrowed as he studied the figure. He had the ability to jump through time, but this man—this henchman—had been sent from a future Rishab couldn't fully comprehend. The **future Moksha** envisioned, where his dominion over time was absolute. The very thought unsettled Rishab, and he clenched his fists, feeling the weight of the **ancient battles** that now seemed so distant. This wasn't just a war for dominance—**Moksha was playing with the fabric of reality itself.**

Rishab (in thought):

If he's from the future, he knows things we don't. He knows what happens next—and that gives him an advantage. I have to find a way to counter it.

Indra clicked another button, and the screen shifted to display another figure. This time, the image was sharper—an older man with **sharp, intelligent eyes**, standing in what appeared to be a high-tech laboratory. The lab was filled with advanced equipment—machinery and devices that seemed far too **futuristic** for the present day. There was something sinister about the way the man's fingers lingered on a control panel, as if he were crafting a masterpiece of destruction.

Indra:

*"The second henchman is a scientist. His name is **Dr. Keshava**. He's been working on a machine that will allow Moksha to create a **stable two-way portal** between the future and the present. Currently, Moksha can only bring small amounts of energy and his henchmen through the portal, powered by the blood of the Immortals. But Keshava's machine—if completed—will allow Moksha to bring **entire armies** from the future into the present."*

Rishab's heart sank at the thought. The **blood of the seven Immortals**, the ancient force that had been used to create this time breach, was already powerful beyond comprehension. But if this scientist succeeded in his task, **Moksha would no longer be constrained by the limitations of the portal**. He could summon an **unstoppable army from the future**, bringing with him weapons and technology far beyond anything that existed in the present day. This wasn't just a battle—it was a war across time itself.

Reet stepped forward, her brow furrowed in thought. The image of the scientist seemed to ignite something in her—a mixture of **frustration** and **determination**. She had seen men like him before—minds that were too brilliant for their own good, capable of creating miracles or disasters with equal ease.

Reet (grimly):

"If he succeeds, we won't just be fighting Moksha. We'll be facing an army that's already conquered the future. We'll be fighting a war that's already been won."

Roshan crossed his arms, his expression hardening. His frustration was palpable, and Rishab could see the fire of determination in his eyes. Roshan was a man of action, not one to sit idly by while the world burned around him.

Roshan (gruffly):

"Then we need to stop them before they get any closer. We can't let Moksha gain any more ground. This time-traveler—how do we find him?"

***Indra let out a sigh**, the weight of the situation pressing heavily on his shoulders. He turned to face the team fully, his posture rigid with the responsibility of centuries of protection. This wasn't just another mission—**this was their last chance**.*

Indra:

"We've been tracking the time-traveler's movements. He's clever—always staying one step ahead of us. But we believe he's targeting a specific weapon—something that was buried centuries ago. It's a relic of immense power, one of the last few that Moksha needs for his machine. If the time-traveler finds it and delivers it to Moksha, they'll have everything they need to rewrite history."

Rishab's mind raced. **The convergence of past and future** was happening faster than any of them had anticipated. The **relics of ancient power**, the future technology, the blood of the Immortals—it was all coming together to create a **perfect storm**, and Moksha was the eye of it. Rishab's memories of his past lives, the battles he had fought against Moksha in each incarnation, swirled in his mind again. He had always been able to stop Moksha before, but this time was different. **This wasn't just about strength or skill—this was about time itself.**

Rishab (firmly):

"Then let's move quickly. We can't let them gain any more ground."

Indra nodded, but his eyes remained fixed on Rishab, the mistrust still lingering just beneath the surface. He was a man who had seen betrayal, who had watched as the **best warriors in history** had fallen to the allure of power. **Rishab's immense strength** made him both a valuable asset and a potential threat. Indra's jaw tightened slightly as he spoke again, the weight of his words pressing down on the room.

Indra (coldly):

"We need more than speed. We need to find the weapon before they do, or everything we've done to protect this world will be for nothing. If Moksha gets the last four relics, he'll have all the power he needs to complete the machine and rewrite history."

The gravity of his words settled heavily over the room. **Roshan**, always quick to act, was visibly impatient, his fists clenching and unclenching as he awaited the signal to move. **Reet**, while more composed, stood deep in thought, clearly calculating their next move. Rishab, though outwardly composed, felt a surge of anxiety creeping in. **This was bigger than anything he had ever faced**.

For the first time in a long while, **Rishab doubted himself**. The **time-jumping technology** Moksha possessed was far beyond anything Rishab had encountered in his past lives. How could he counter something designed to manipulate the very fabric of time itself?

As if sensing his unease, **Reet spoke up**, her voice steady and reassuring.

Reet (calmly):

"We have to think ahead. If the time-traveler has access to future knowledge, we'll need to be smarter, faster, and more strategic than ever. Rishab, you have the ability to jump through time too. Maybe that's the key. You can anticipate their moves."

Rishab nodded, though doubt still clouded his mind. **His time-jumping abilities** had always been linked to his deep meditation, to his connection with the universe. He wasn't sure how well he could control them under the pressure of battle. But **Reet was right**. They needed every advantage they could get, and if his abilities could help, he had to try.

Rishab (determined):

"I'll do whatever it takes. If my time-jumping can help us predict their moves, then I'll use it."

Roshan grunted in agreement, his voice rough with determination.

Roshan:

"Then it's settled. We track this time-traveler, and we stop him before he finds the weapon. We can't let Moksha win."

Indra turned back to the screens, bringing up a map of their target. It was a dense jungle, far to the east, littered with ancient temples and forgotten relics. The location glowed faintly on the screen, a **marker of power** and danger.

Indra:

"We have a lead on the time-traveler's next location. It's an ancient site, tied to the weapon we believe he's after. If we move quickly, we can intercept him before he reaches it. But be prepared—Moksha's forces are unpredictable. We'll need to expect the unexpected."

The room buzzed with anticipation. **Rishab's mind raced** as he studied the map, the weight of the coming battle pressing heavily on his shoulders. **He had faced Moksha across lifetimes**, but this was different. This was a war for time itself. One mistake, one moment of hereettion, and everything they had fought for could be lost.

Rishab (in thought):

I've stopped him before. I can stop him again. But this time... I can't do it alone.

The tension in the room was palpable as the team prepared to move. **Roshan and Reet** gathered their weapons, their faces etched with grim determination. **Indra's gaze remained fixed on Rishab**, his expression unreadable. Despite Rishab's confidence, the shadow of mistrust still lingered between them. **Indra had seen too many warriors fall to arrogance and power**, and he wasn't willing to trust Rishab fully—not yet.

As the team filed out of the room, **Rishab stole one last glance at the screen**. The images of Moksha's henchmen loomed over him, a reminder that the battle ahead would test not only his strength but his **mind** and his **control** over the powers he had been given.

The war for time had begun.

Chapter 9

The Battle That Never Ended

The city was alive with sound—a continuous, frenetic pulse of life humming through its streets. **Neon lights flickered overhead**, casting a kaleidoscope of colors onto the glass buildings that towered high into the sky. Hovering vehicles zipped through the air, and the chatter of pedestrians melded with the distant hum of machinery. But beneath the vibrant exterior, there was a tension—an underlying current that spoke of something **darker lurking just out of sight.**

Moving with purpose through the throngs of people were **Rishab**, **Roshan**, and **Reet**, their faces hidden beneath hoods, blending into the urban chaos. They had been tracking **Moksha's forces** for weeks, piecing together information that led them here—**to the heart of the city**, where one of Moksha's henchmen was rumored to be hiding. The ancient weapon they sought was somewhere inside an old industrial building, a **relic lost to time**, now sitting like a forgotten ghost amidst the sleek, modern skyline.

The once-thriving factory was now a hollowed-out shell, its windows shattered and its machinery rusting. It had been abandoned for decades, but according to **Indra's intelligence**, it now held a relic that could tip the balance in Moksha's favor. If his forces retrieved it, the consequences would be catastrophic. Rishab felt the weight of the mission pressing down on him, the urgency pushing his every step. **There was no room for failure.**

As they neared the building, **Roshan's muscles tensed**, his fists clenching and unclenching beneath his jacket. The distant sound of gunfire echoed through the air, followed by the sharp clash of metal on metal.

Roshan (growling):

"Looks like the party's already started."

Reet, ever calm and calculating, adjusted her **high-tech goggles**. The lenses flickered as they scanned the area, mapping the battlefield ahead.

Reet (grimly):

"There's another group in play. We're not the only ones after the weapon."

Through the haze of dust and broken machinery, **Rishab's eyes focused on the shadows moving inside the building**. He could make out two groups—one clearly **Moksha's henchmen**, led by a man in futuristic armor. The other group appeared to be **mercenaries**, heavily armed and engaged in a brutal firefight with Moksha's forces. This wasn't just a mission to retrieve a relic—**it was a full-scale battle**.

Rishab (in thought):

Moksha's henchmen... and another faction. This complicates things.

Rishab turned to **Roshan**, whose jaw was clenched, his eyes gleaming with the anticipation of battle. His fists shook, brimming with barely contained fury, but **Rishab knew they had to keep a clear head**. This mission wasn't just about brute force—it was about strategy. They couldn't afford mistakes.

Rishab (determined):

"We'll use the chaos to our advantage. We move in while they're distracted. No unnecessary risks."

Roshan cracked his knuckles, a wild grin spreading across his face. He thrived in the heat of battle, but his recklessness was a double-edged sword.

Roshan (grinning):

"Let's do it. I've been itching for a fight."

They moved quickly, splitting up to cover more ground. **Reet** moved with precision, setting up traps and calibrating her equipment as they advanced. **Rishab's mind was razor-sharp**, his senses heightened as he approached the building. **The sounds of battle** grew louder, and his heart raced.

For **Rishab**, battle was second nature. He had done this before—**across lifetimes, across eras.** His past lives echoed in his mind, reminding him of battles fought with swords, spears, and magic. Each lifetime had prepared him for this moment, but now he had something he hadn't had in the past—**allies.** Roshan's brute strength and Reet's tactical genius would be essential.

As they reached the perimeter, the scene unfolded before them. **Moksha's henchmen**, led by the **time-traveler**, were locked in combat with the **mercenaries**, their bodies and weapons crashing against each other with ferocity. Bullets ricocheted off the walls, and bright energy blasts streaked across the battlefield, creating a cacophony of destruction.

The time-traveler, clad in his futuristic armor, moved with terrifying precision. He dodged attacks effortlessly, as if he knew where each strike would land before it even began. **His armor pulsed with energy**, a faint glow emanating from the intricate designs that adorned it, powered by technology far beyond anything from the present day.

Rishab (in thought, narrowing his eyes):

That's what we're up against. He's from the future... He knows things we can't predict.

The realization sent a chill through Rishab's spine. He had fought **Moksha's forces** in countless lifetimes, but never against a foe with this kind of **future insight**. This wasn't just a battle—it was a war against time itself.

Roshan, however, was already charging ahead, his muscles swelling as his **rage fueled him**. He was a force of nature, smashing through the mercenaries with raw power. Bodies flew into the air as **Roshan's fists connected with bone and metal**, his every movement radiating destruction. But as much as his strength was an asset, Rishab could see the lack of control in Roshan's attacks.

Rishab (shouting to Roshan):

"Stay focused! Don't let the rage control you!"

But **Roshan** was already lost in the fight. He tore through the battlefield like a hurricane, plowing into the **time-traveler** with a blow that made the man stagger. For a moment, **Roshan's overwhelming strength** seemed like it would win the day, but just as quickly, the **time-traveler vanished** in a flash of light.

He reappeared a few feet away, his movements impossibly fast. **Roshan's furious strike** had hit only air.

Reet (urgently):

"Roshan! He's time-jumping! Be careful!"

The **time-traveler's time-jumping** allowed him to rewrite moments, **flashing back and forth through time** to change the immediate past. Each movement seemed to be part of a carefully crafted strategy, designed to confuse and overwhelm. **Rishab's heart pounded** as he watched Roshan's attacks grow more erratic.

Rishab (in thought, worried):

Roshan's losing control. I have to rein him in, or we'll lose this fight.

STAY FOCUSE!!
DON'T LET THE FAGE
FANT COYTFEL YOU!

Reet, meanwhile, had taken position at the edge of the battlefield, using her **tech-savvy mind** to stay one step ahead. She had already hacked into the **time-traveler's communication systems**, disrupting his link to Moksha. Her eyes darted between her equipment and the battle, her mind calculating probabilities and setting traps along the perimeter. She wasn't a fighter like Rishab or Roshan, but she was every bit as dangerous.

With a final keystroke, **Reet disabled the time-traveler's advanced tech shield**, causing a flicker of disruption in his armor.

Reet (calmly):

"Rishab, I've hacked into his suit. He's vulnerable now."

Rishab nodded. They had an opening, but it wouldn't last long.

Rishab took a deep breath, activating the **chip in his chest**. His ability to **manipulate time** came with a heavy price—it required complete focus and meditation. He felt time slow as his senses heightened, the world around him becoming a blur of sound and motion. **He could see the paths of attacks before they happened**, the future unfolding before his eyes like a well-mapped out strategy.

In this heightened state, **Rishab moved through the chaos with ease**, dodging bullets and strikes as though they were moving in slow motion. He materialized behind mercenaries and **Moksha's henchmen**, taking them out with swift, calculated blows. Every movement was precise—**he was a warrior from countless lives**, honed by centuries of battle.

Roshan (roaring):

"Rishab, over here!"

Roshan's voice was a roar over the cacophony of battle. Rishab turned just in time to see **Roshan smashing through a group of mercenaries**, his raw power sending shockwaves through the ground. But as Roshan swung at the **time-traveler** again, the man vanished once more, **time-jumping** to avoid the blow.

Rishab's mind raced. The **time-traveler's control over time** was as dangerous as his strength. Every time he jumped, he altered the immediate past, avoiding attacks and changing the course of battle. **Rishab needed to anticipate his next jump** before it happened.

Rishab (in thought, focused):

I can see it—he's jumping into the past. I just need to time it right.

As the **time-traveler reappeared**, **Rishab was ready**. His heightened senses allowed him to anticipate the jump, and before the time-traveler could strike, **Rishab attacked**, landing a blow that sent the man stumbling back. But the time-traveler was quick to recover, his eyes gleaming with confidence.

Time-Traveler (smirking):

"You're too late. This weapon belongs to Moksha now."

Rishab clenched his fists, feeling the energy surge through him. His past lives whispered in his mind, guiding him.

Rishab (fiercely):

"I've fought Moksha before. I've stopped him in every lifetime. This will be no different."

The **time-traveler laughed**, a cold, calculating sound. His eyes glinted with the knowledge of someone who had seen the future.

Time-Traveler (mocking):

"We'll see about that."

The two clashed, their **movements a blur** of speed and power. **Both men used their time-jumping abilities**, shifting through space in a deadly dance. The fight was a test of skill, strategy, and instinct, with neither able to gain the upper hand for long. **Rishab's past lives guided his every move**, but the time-traveler fought with a precision that bordered on inhuman.

Meanwhile, outside the building, the battle raged on. **Roshan's fury** had reached its peak, his attacks becoming more devastating by the second. But **Reet**, watching from her position, saw the toll it was taking on him. **Roshan's rage was clouding his judgment**—he was losing control.

Reet (yelling to Roshan):

"Stay in control! Don't let the anger take over!"

Back inside, the fight between **Rishab and the time-traveler** reached its climax. **Rishab's breathing was labored**, sweat dripping down his face as he fought to maintain focus. But he could see it—the **time-traveler's next move**. With a burst of energy, **Rishab anticipated**

the jump, landing a devastating blow that sent the time-traveler crashing into the wall.

But before Rishab could finish him, **the time-traveler vanished** once again, disappearing into the fabric of time.

Rishab stood alone, his chest heaving, the battle momentarily paused. Before him, the **ancient weapon**—the relic they had been fighting for—glowed ominously in the dim light. He had won this round, but **Moksha's forces would return**.

Rishab (breathing heavily):

"We stopped them for now, but Moksha will be back. This is just the beginning."

As the team regrouped, the weight of their mission settled over them. They had succeeded in preventing the weapon from falling into **Moksha's hands**, but the fight ahead would only grow more dangerous. **Trust and teamwork** had gotten them this far, but they would need even more to stop the forces that were coming.

The war for **time had only just begun**.

Chapter 10

Victory and Consequences

The dust of battle hung in the air like a heavy fog, settling slowly over the wreckage of the old factory. For a brief moment, the world seemed to still—**a fragile silence** after the chaos of the fight. Rishab stood amidst the debris, his chest rising and falling with each labored breath, his muscles still twitching with the aftershocks of adrenaline. **His eyes swept over the battlefield**, taking in the bodies of the fallen and the destruction they had wrought. The fight had been brutal, testing the limits of his strength and endurance, but they had emerged victorious. Or so he thought.

As **Roshan** and **Reet** approached him, their expressions grim, **Rishab's gaze locked on the vault** where the ancient weapon had been hidden. The massive steel door, once thought impenetrable, had been forced open, its hinges twisted and broken. **A hollow silence greeted him** from within the chamber, the absence of the relic a **stark and painful reminder** of Moksha's cunning.

Reet (grimly, her voice barely a whisper):

"He's already taken it."

Roshan, leaning heavily on his staff for support, cursed under his breath. Blood trickled down his arm from a deep wound he had sustained during the fight, his face pale and lined with pain. His breathing was labored, each inhale ragged and uneven, but **his spirit remained defiant**.

Roshan (through gritted teeth):

"We fought hard... but we still lost what we came for."

Rishab's expression darkened as his eyes fixed on the empty vault. Despite the intense battle and the victory they had achieved by defeating one of **Moksha's henchmen**, the sense of accomplishment felt hollow. The ancient weapon, the very thing they had risked their lives to secure, was gone—**now in Moksha's hands**.

This wasn't just a loss; it was a catastrophic blow to their mission. The weapon was more than just a relic. It was **a key piece of Moksha's plan** to rewrite history and bend time to his will. And they had failed to stop him.

Rishab (in thought, his fists clenching):

Moksha... he's always one step ahead. How does he do it?

The weight of their failure pressed down on Rishab's shoulders, heavier than any sword or armor he had carried in his countless past lives. **Every time they seemed to gain ground**, Moksha found a way to **slip through their fingers**, leaving destruction and chaos in his wake. **How could they hope to defeat him**, when he had control over time itself?

But the sound of **Roshan's labored breathing** pulled him back to the present. **Roshan's injuries were far worse** than they had initially realized. Blood soaked his shirt, pooling on the ground beneath him, and his steps were unsteady. **The wound was deep**, and Rishab could see the strain it was putting on his friend's body.

Reet (her voice rising in panic):

"Roshan! You're hurt—badly."

Roshan waved her off, his pride refusing to let him admit just how much pain he was in. His brow was slick with sweat, his jaw clenched tight, but **Rishab could see the truth**—Roshan wouldn't last much longer without help.

Roshan (through gasping breaths, trying to smile):

"I'll be fine... just a scratch."

But the blood soaking through his clothes told a different story. Rishab's heart tightened with urgency. **Roshan was more than just a fighter**—he was a brother to him in all but blood, and Rishab knew that losing him would be more than a personal loss. It would **shatter the fragile balance** that held their team together. They couldn't afford to lose him now, not when the stakes were so high.

Rishab (urgently, his voice hard with determination):

"We need the Sanjivani Booti. It's our only chance. Only that herb can heal a wound from a mythical weapon like this."

Reet's eyes widened at the mention of the ancient herb. The **Sanjivani Booti**—a legendary plant said to have healing properties so powerful that it could even bring the dead back to life. In the tales of old, it had been used to save warriors on the brink of death, but it was not an easy thing to find. The herb was rare, hidden deep within the most dangerous mountains, and **guarded by ancient forces**.

Reet (determined, nodding):

"Then we don't have a choice. We have to find it. Roshan won't survive much longer without it."

Rishab looked down at **Roshan**, whose face had grown even paler. **Time was slipping away**, and every second they wasted was another moment Roshan's life hung in the balance. **The battle had been taxing**, pushing them all to their limits, but now was not the time to rest. They had to act quickly, or all would be lost.

Rishab (steeling himself, his mind racing):

"We move now. No hereettion."

As they began to regroup, **Rishab glanced back at the fallen henchman**—the **time-traveler** who had fought with such deadly precision. The man's body lay still, but even in death, his presence was a **grim reminder of Moksha's reach**. This henchman had been from the future, armed with knowledge and technology far beyond their understanding. If this was just one of **Moksha's pawns**, what other horrors awaited them?

Rishab (in thought, his fists tightening):

The fight isn't over. It's only just begun. We can't afford to fail again.

Roshan groaned in pain, clutching his side as **Reet knelt beside him**, her eyes filled with concern. The urgency of the situation pulled Rishab back from his thoughts. There was no time for reflection—not now.

Rishab (his voice firm, filled with determination):

"Let's go. We'll save Roshan, and then we'll deal with Moksha."

With **Reet's help**, Roshan was lifted to his feet, though his steps were shaky, his body barely able to support his own weight. **Every movement seemed to worsen his condition**, but Roshan, ever the warrior, gritted his teeth and pressed forward. They moved quickly out of the ruined building, heading toward their next destination—the mountains where the **Sanjivani Booti** was rumored to grow. The city lights faded behind them as they ventured into the wilderness, the victory they had tasted now **bittersweet and hollow**.

The battle had been won, but at a terrible cost. **The weapon was gone**, and Roshan's life hung in the balance. They had defeated one of **Moksha's henchmen**, but **their failure to secure the relic** was a stark reminder that Moksha was still out there—plotting, moving, always one step ahead.

The mission had shifted. It was no longer about retrieving the weapon—it was about **survival**.

Reet (glancing at Rishab, her voice low):

"How far are we from the mountains? Do you think... do you think we'll make it in time?"

Rishab's jaw clenched. He didn't have the answer she was looking for. **The Sanjivani Booti was more than just a legend**—it was their only hope. But it wasn't just finding it that worried him. The herb was guarded, hidden away by forces that had existed for centuries, forces that had sworn to protect its power from falling into the wrong hands.

Rishab (quietly, his eyes hard with resolve):

"We'll make it. We have to."

Roshan's breathing grew more labored as they trekked deeper into the wilderness, the **light from the city long behind them**. The road ahead was treacherous, filled with uneven ground and narrow paths that wound up into the towering mountains. **The air grew colder**, biting at their skin as the altitude increased, and the landscape became more dangerous with every step.

Rishab's thoughts raced as he led the way, his mind filled with images of Moksha—**his past lives colliding with the present**. He had faced Moksha before, across countless incarnations, but this time felt different. **Moksha's mastery over time** had turned the rules of the game upside down. He wasn't just altering the future—**he was rewriting history itself**.

As they climbed higher, **Reet's hand tightened around Roshan's**, trying to keep him steady as his body weakened.

Roshan (his voice hoarse, barely audible):

"Rishab... I... I'm sorry. I should've... been stronger."

Rishab stopped, turning to face his brother-in-arms. Roshan's face was pale, his body trembling from the effort of staying upright. The sight of him like this—**so vulnerable, so unlike the indomitable warrior he usually was**—cut deep into Rishab's heart.

Rishab (his voice firm, yet filled with compassion):

"You've fought harder than anyone else, Roshan. There's no shame in being hurt. We'll find the Sanjivani Booti, and you'll be back on your feet in no time."

Roshan smiled weakly, though it was clear he was struggling to hold on.

Reet (urgently):

"We need to keep moving. The longer we stay here, the worse it'll get."

With renewed urgency, the group pressed on. The path became **steeper and more treacherous**, the jagged rocks cutting into their hands as they climbed higher. **The wind howled** through the mountains, carrying with it an eerie silence, as if the world was holding its breath.

And then, after hours of grueling travel, they reached a plateau—**a hidden valley nestled between the peaks**. In the center of the valley was a single tree, **glowing with an ethereal light**, its branches laden with leaves of a deep emerald hue. **The Sanjivani Booti**.

Reet (in awe, her voice soft):

"We found it..."

But **Rishab's instincts flared**. The valley, though seemingly serene, was not unguarded. Ancient forces had protected the Sanjivani Booti for centuries, and they would not give it up without a fight.

Rishab (quietly, his eyes scanning the surroundings):

"We're not alone. Be ready."

As they approached the tree, **the ground trembled**, and from the shadows emerged figures—**guardians of the Sanjivani Booti**, their forms towering and menacing, their eyes glowing with ancient power.

Roshan (through gritted teeth, his hand on his weapon):

"Here we go again."

Rishab's eyes narrowed. They had faced impossible odds before, and they would do so again. The fight for Roshan's life had begun, and they would not leave without the herb.

Chapter 11

The First Fracture

The air around Rishab shimmered, the familiar pull of time bending as the chip embedded in his chest activated. It was a sensation he had grown accustomed to—the fabric of reality warping as he was drawn through the strands of time. But this journey was different. This wasn't about facing a powerful foe or altering the course of a battle from his past lives. This was about saving Roshan, his closest friend and brother in arms, from death's grip.

The present dissolved, and before him emerged the lush, vibrant jungle of the Rishabayana era. Dense, ancient trees stretched skyward, their towering canopies alive with a magical energy. The air was thick with the scent of earth and mystery, and the golden-red hues of the sky created an otherworldly glow over the land. It was as if time itself had slowed, allowing Rishab to soak in the moment.

Rishab (in thought, his gaze scanning the ancient landscape):

The Sanjivani Booti is here somewhere. I've heard the stories... but finding it will be anything but easy.

The Sanjivani Booti was not just any herb—it was a legendary plant, believed to possess miraculous healing properties capable of reviving those on the brink of death. It had once saved Roshan during the great battle of the Rishabayana, when Lord Rishab and Hanuman had ventured into this very jungle to find it. Centuries had passed, but the myth of the herb persisted. Now, Rishab found himself retracing the footsteps of his divine predecessor, his heart heavy with urgency.

The jungle around him pulsed with ancient power. Every leaf, every branch, seemed to hum with life, as if guarding secrets long buried. Rishab moved cautiously, aware that he was treading on sacred ground. This wasn't just a physical journey—it was a spiritual one, testing not only his strength but his heart.

His footsteps barely made a sound, but the jungle was alive with whispers. Birds fluttered overhead, their calls echoing like warnings. Creatures of legend watched from the shadows, their eyes glowing faintly, though none dared reveal themselves fully. Rishab's senses were on high alert, his instincts sharpened by the memories of countless battles fought across time.

Suddenly, the ground shifted beneath him. With lightning reflexes, Rishab leaped back just in time to avoid a massive stone slab that crashed down from the trees, narrowly missing him. The trap had been well-hidden, and for a brief moment, Rishab's heart raced. He was no stranger to danger, but this jungle was unlike anything he had encountered before.

Rishab (in thought, his body tensing):

This place is protected—just as I expected. I'll need to be more cautious.

As he continued his trek deeper into the jungle, the challenges grew more dangerous. Rishab narrowly dodged more booby traps—poison darts hidden in the trees, falling rocks, and even shifting paths that seemed designed to lead him in circles. Yet, his mind remained focused, his heart steady. He knew that these obstacles were not just tests of his strength but of his willpower and perseverance.

As Rishab rounded a bend, he felt a powerful presence watching him. The air around him thickened, vibrating with a force that made the hairs on his neck stand on end. From the shadows, a massive figure emerged—its silhouette imposing against the backdrop of the jungle. Jambavan, the mighty bear king, stepped forward, his fur shimmering with an otherworldly light. His eyes gleamed with wisdom and ancient knowledge, a presence that carried the weight of millennia.

Jambavan (his voice deep, rumbling like thunder):

"You travel through time, yet your heart carries the burdens of many lives. What is it that you seek, traveler?"

Rishab's breath caught in his throat. He had heard the stories of Jambavan, the ally of Lord Rishab and Hanuman, the one who had fought in the great battles of the Rishabayana. To meet him now—after centuries had passed—felt like stepping into the pages of history itself. Respectfully, Rishab bowed his head.

Rishab (respectfully, his voice steady):

"Jambavan, I seek the Sanjivani Booti. A dear friend's life hangs in the balance, just as it did in the time of Lord Rishab. I need your guidance."

Jambavan's eyes narrowed, as if peering into Rishab's soul. He stood still, towering over Rishab, his presence both commanding and calm. After a long pause, the ancient bear king nodded, though the expression on his face was one of quiet contemplation.

Jambavan (gravelly, his voice filled with centuries of experience):

"The Sanjivani Booti is not given to those who merely seek it. It must be earned, and the trials ahead are treacherous. Many have tried, but few have succeeded."

Rishab met his gaze, his expression resolute. He wasn't here for glory, nor was he here for personal gain. He was here to save Roshan, to fulfill a promise. His determination burned bright, even in the face of the legendary figure standing before him.

Rishab (his voice unwavering):

"I will face whatever trials lie ahead, no matter the cost."

Jambavan studied him for another long moment before stepping aside, his massive form moving with the grace of a seasoned warrior. He motioned for Rishab to follow, and together, they ventured deeper into the jungle. The path ahead was perilous, filled with wild creatures lurking in the shadows, ancient traps designed to confuse and disorient, and even the very landscape itself shifting beneath their feet.

But with Jambavan's guidance and Rishab's own experience from countless lifetimes, they pressed on, never wavering.

As they traveled, Rishab's thoughts turned inward. He had faced countless battles in his past lives, but this journey was different. He wasn't fighting for himself—he was fighting for someone he loved. His bond with Roshan was one forged in countless struggles, and as the memories of his past lives resurfaced, Rishab realized something profound: He had never been alone in his battles. He had always had allies, brothers-in-arms, friends who fought beside him, who shared his burden.

Rishab (in thought, reflecting on his past): *I've fought Moksha across lifetimes, but I've never been alone. I've always had allies by my side, even when the battle seemed impossible. Roshan... Reet... Jambavan... they are my strength.*

The deeper they ventured into the jungle, the more treacherous the path became. The air grew colder, the trees twisted into unnatural shapes, and the hum of magic intensified. But finally, after what seemed like hours of navigating the dangerous terrain, they reached the base of a towering mountain.

At the peak of the mountain, the Sanjiavani Booti glowed faintly, bathed in the golden light of the setting sun. But between them and the herb stood a formidable obstacle—a colossal serpent, coiled around the mountain, its scales shimmering with ancient magic, its eyes glowing with a fierce, otherworldly light. The serpent's presence was suffocating, its gaze fixed on Rishab and Jambavan as they approached.

Serpent Guardian (hissing, its voice cold and echoing):

"Only the worthy may claim the Sanjivani Booti. Prove yourself, or be destroyed."

Rishab's muscles tensed, his mind sharpening as he prepared for battle. This was the final trial, the ultimate test of his strength, heart, and resolve. The serpent's massive form shifted as it coiled tighter around the mountain, its tail swishing through the air with deadly intent. The ground shook beneath Rishab's feet, and he knew this battle would require not only his physical prowess but also the lessons he had learned across lifetimes.

Jambavan (calmly, his eyes filled with wisdom):

"Remember, Rishab—it is not just strength that will win this battle, but the strength of your heart."

The serpent struck first, its tail whipping through the air with the speed of lightning. Rishab dodged the attack, rolling to the side as the tail slammed into the ground where he had just stood. The impact created a crater, dust rising into the air.

Rishab's heart pounded, but he remained calm, using his time-jumping ability to predict the serpent's next move. He saw the serpent coil back, preparing for another strike, and in the blink of an eye, Rishab vanished from where he stood, reappearing several feet away just as the serpent's fangs snapped at the air where he had been.

The battle was fierce, the serpent moving with deadly precision. Its attacks were relentless, each strike intended to crush Rishab beneath its massive weight. But Rishab's time-jumping ability allowed him to stay one step ahead, dodging the serpent's attacks with swift movements. Yet, he knew that avoiding the blows wouldn't be enough. He had to find an opening—a weakness.

The serpent's eyes glowed brighter, and its body coiled tighter around the mountain, creating a suffocating wall of scales. It hissed, its voice filled with venom.

Serpent Guardian (mocking):

"You think you can defeat me, mortal? I have guarded this mountain for centuries. You are nothing but a fleeting moment in time."

Rishab clenched his fists, his determination growing stronger. He had faced challenges far greater than this. He had fought Moksha's forces across countless eras. He had defeated enemies with powers far beyond imagination. This serpent was just another trial—another step in his journey.

Rishab (in thought, his resolve hardening):

I am not just a mortal. I carry the strength of my past lives, the wisdom of my allies. I will not fail.

The serpent lunged again, but this time, Rishab was ready. He shifted through time, appearing behind the serpent and striking with precision. The serpent let out a roar of pain, its body recoiling as Rishab landed another blow. The battle raged on, with each clash testing Rishab's endurance and resolve. But slowly, he began to wear the serpent down, his strikes becoming more calculated, his movements more fluid.

Finally, after what felt like hours, Rishab saw an opening. The serpent reared back, preparing for a final, devastating strike, but Rishab moved faster. With a surge of strength, he leaped into the air, his fist glowing with energy, and struck the serpent at its vulnerable spot—the base of its neck.

The serpent let out a final roar, its body collapsing in defeat. The air grew still, the glow of the Sanjivani Booti growing brighter as the guardian retreated, acknowledging Rishab's victory.

Rishab (panting, his chest heaving):

"It's over..."

Jambavan stepped forward, his expression filled with quiet pride as he approached Rishab. The battle had been won, but the journey was far from over.

Jambavan (gravelly, with wisdom):

"You have proven yourself worthy, Rishab. The Sanjivani Booti will heal your friend, but never forget—your greatest strength comes not from power, but from the unity of those who stand beside you."

Rishab carefully plucked the Sanjivani Booti, the herb's soft glow filling him with a sense of peace. He had succeeded, but more importantly, he had been reminded of the strength that came from within—and from the bonds he had forged with his allies.

With the herb in hand, Rishab turned to Jambavan, bowing his head in gratitude.

Rishab (with gratitude):

"Thank you, Jambavan. I couldn't have done this without you."

Jambavan nodded, his eyes filled with ancient wisdom as Rishab began his journey back to the present. As the jungle around him dissolved, replaced by the familiar sights of his own time, Rishab felt a renewed sense of purpose.

Rishab (in thought, determined):

Roshan's life will be saved, and together, we will stop Moksha. No battle is impossible when you fight with those you trust by your side.

The fight against Moksha was far from over, but with the Sanjivani Booti in his grasp and the lessons of unity in his heart, Rishab knew that he was ready for whatever came next.

Chapter 12

Resurrection Protocol

The heavy air within the Chirayu Foundation's base mirrored the weight of the emotions that hung thick in the atmosphere. Time had become a cruel tormentor, stretching the moments into an unbearable silence. Reet sat beside Roshan, who lay unconscious, his once formidable body now fragile and weakened by the severity of his injuries. She glanced at his face, usually so full of life and fire, now pale, his breath shallow and labored.

A deep sense of fear gripped her heart. **Roshan**, the indomitable warrior who had charged fearlessly into countless battles, now lay on the edge of death. His breathing, once strong and steady, was now a faint whisper. Every second felt like an eternity. The tension among the team grew with each moment that passed without Rishab's return.

Indra stood in the shadows, his arms crossed, watching the scene with a mix of concern and skepticism. While the others prayed for Rishab's success, a part of Indra remained doubtful. The **Sanjivani Booti** was a mythical herb, its existence steeped in legend. Could Rishab really retrieve it? Indra's mind wrestled with questions about their mission and the price they were paying in their fight against Moksha.

The sun had begun to dip lower in the sky, casting long shadows across the base, when a ripple of energy vibrated through the air. A sudden, sharp crack echoed in the distance, and the team turned their heads toward the entrance. There, standing tall with a grim yet determined expression, was Rishab. His clothes were dusty from the ancient jungle, his skin shimmering slightly from the energy of the time-jumping journey. But what drew everyone's attention was the soft glow in his hand—**the Sanjivani Booti**.

Reet (her voice breaking with relief):

"Rishab! You found it—please, we don't have much time."

Rishab nodded, the weariness from his journey evident in his eyes. He moved swiftly toward Roshan, whose body lay still on the bed of woven fabric. The sight of his brother-like friend, reduced to such a fragile state, sent a wave of emotion surging through Rishab's chest. **Roshan**, who had always been the unstoppable force in their battles, was now so close to the brink of death. His mind raced as he knelt beside Roshan, clenching the glowing herb tightly in his hand.

Rishab (in thought, his gaze softening as he looked at Roshan):

I can't fail him. Not now. Not after everything we've been through.

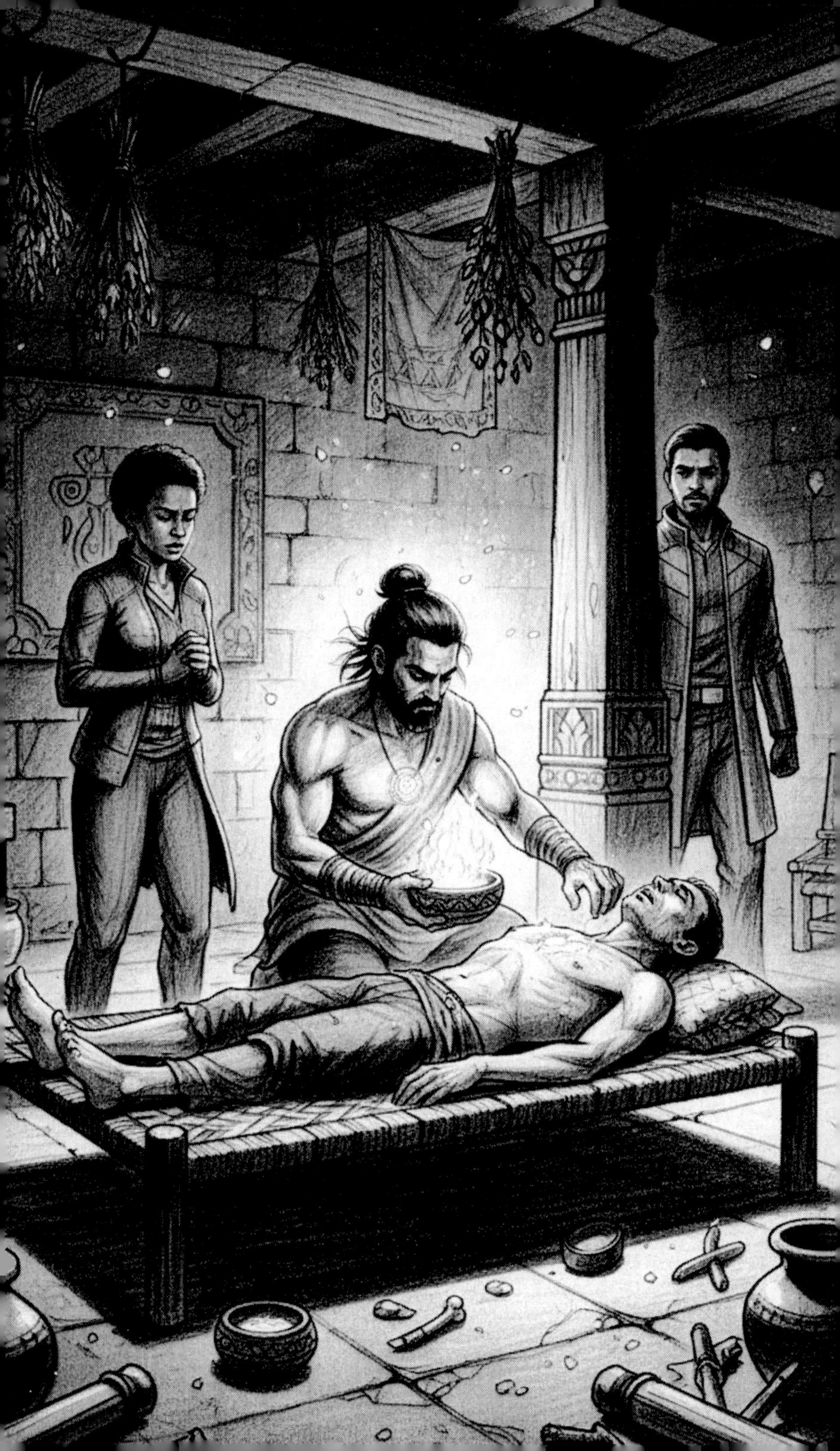

Rishab had fought so many battles, faced so many enemies across countless lifetimes, but this moment was different. **This wasn't about defeating a foe; it was about saving the life of someone he loved.**

Rishab took a deep breath, forcing himself to remain calm and steady. He placed the **Sanjivani Booti** on a clean cloth in front of him and began to work. His hands moved with deliberate care, grinding the precious herb into a paste. As he did, ancient rituals from his past lives came flooding back to him—**sacred chants**, forgotten prayers, and the deep knowledge of healing that transcended time. The memories guided his hands as he prepared the medicine with precision, drawing on the energies that flowed through him.

Around him, the team watched in silence, their hearts gripped by a mix of hope and fear. **Reet** stood closest, her face lined with exhaustion and worry. She had fought alongside Roshan for years, through every battle, always trusting in his strength. But seeing him like this, so close to death, shook her to the core.

Indra, too, had stepped forward from the shadows, his skeptical nature momentarily softened by the gravity of the situation. He observed Rishab closely, the herbal paste glowing faintly under the dim light of the room. The air was thick with tension, every breath filled with the unspoken fear that this might be Roshan's last.

Rishab (his voice soft but filled with quiet power):

"May the forces that guide life, the energy that heals, and the power of the Sanjivani bring Roshan back to us."

Rishab's words hung in the air, carrying with them an ancient resonance. It was more than a prayer—it was a command, an invocation of the energies of the universe to breathe life back into Roshan. The room seemed to vibrate with the energy of Rishab's voice, the air itself shimmering as if the forces of nature were responding to his call.

With gentle hands, Rishab applied the **Sanjivani Booti** paste to Roshan's wound, his movements precise, his focus unwavering. The glowing paste spread across the injury, and for a long moment, nothing happened. The team held their collective breath, the silence in the room so thick it felt as though time itself had stopped.

Then, slowly, **Roshan's chest rose with a deep, shuddering breath**.

Reet (gasping, tears welling in her eyes):

"Roshan... you're back."

Roshan's eyelids fluttered as he struggled to open them, his face still pale but no longer lifeless. His breathing grew stronger, steadier, and the color began to return to his skin. **The power of the Sanjivani Booti** was working, its ancient magic pulling Roshan back from the brink of death.

He blinked, his vision hazy at first, but then focused on the faces around him—Reet's tearful smile, Rishab's exhausted but relieved expression, and the rest of the team, watching with bated breath.

Roshan (his voice hoarse, but with a hint of humor):

"I feel... like I've been hit by a mountain."

A soft laugh rippled through the group, the tension breaking for the first time since the battle. **Even in his weakened state**, Roshan's spirit remained intact. Reet knelt beside him, wiping away tears as she placed a hand on his arm, her relief palpable.

Reet (gently, her voice thick with emotion):

"You gave us quite the scare."

Roshan, still disoriented, looked from Reet to Rishab, his gratitude unspoken but clear in his eyes. He had always been the one to protect others, to charge into danger without hereettion. But now, for the first time in a long while, he had been the one saved. **Rishab**, who had always stood by his side in battle, had once again proven that their bond was unbreakable.

Rishab sat back on his heels, his hands trembling slightly from the toll the journey and the ritual had taken on him. **The Sanjivani Booti's power** had saved Roshan, but it had also drained Rishab's energy. He felt the weight of it all pressing down on him—the weight of their mission, the constant battles, the lives hanging in the balance. For a moment, the relief of victory was overshadowed by the creeping doubt in his mind.

Rishab (in thought, his gaze distant):

How many more times will we face this? How many more battles will push us to the brink?

Victory, once so sweet, now felt fleeting. The joy of Roshan's survival was tempered by the realization that their war against **Moksha** was far from over. **Each battle took a toll**—not just physically, but emotionally. And with every step closer to defeating Moksha, Rishab felt the weight of their mission growing heavier, the stakes higher. **Roshan's near-death experience** was a stark reminder of how fragile life truly was, even for warriors as powerful as they were.

As Roshan sat up with Reet's help, his strength slowly returning, he looked at Rishab with gratitude.

Roshan (his voice still weak, but filled with sincerity):

"Rishab… you saved me again. I owe you my life."

Rishab shook his head, his expression somber. He didn't want Roshan to feel indebted to him—this was not about owing or repaying. **They were brothers** in arms, bound by something far stronger than obligation.

Rishab (quietly, his voice heavy with emotion):

"We're in this together, Roshan. But every battle… it feels like we're paying a price I don't know if we can afford."

Indra, who had been observing the scene with his usual quiet intensity, stepped forward. His voice, though calm, carried the weight of experience.

Indra (firmly, but not unkindly):

"The price of fighting a war like this is always high, Rishab. We all knew that from the beginning. But you did what needed to be done. You saved him, and that's what matters."

Rishab looked up at Indra, meeting his gaze. There was a truth in Indra's words, one that Rishab couldn't deny. **This war against Moksha** had been waged across lifetimes, and every victory had come with a cost. But knowing that didn't ease the burden Rishab felt. **The weight of responsibility** sat heavily on his shoulders, a constant reminder that the battles they fought were far from over.

As Roshan slowly regained his strength, the mood in the room shifted. Relief washed over the group, the bond between them solidified by the near loss of one of their own. For a moment, they allowed themselves to feel the joy of Roshan's recovery, to laugh and smile as they helped him to his feet.

But even in the midst of this small victory, **Rishab's mind couldn't rest**. He knew that **Moksha was still out there**, growing stronger with each passing day. And with the ancient weapon now in Moksha's possession, their next encounter would be even more perilous.

Rishab (in thought, his resolve hardening):

We saved Roshan today. But the fight isn't over. Moksha will come for us again—and next time, the stakes will be higher.

As the group left the room, helping Roshan to rest, **Rishab lingered behind**, his mind swirling with thoughts of what lay ahead. **The Sanjivani Booti** had worked its miracle today, but Rishab knew that they couldn't rely on miracles alone. The war against Moksha was escalating, and every step forward brought them closer to a confrontation that would test not just their strength, but their resolve.

And as the shadows deepened, Rishab vowed to himself that no matter what, he would stand firm in the face of whatever challenges awaited them. **Victory had come at a cost**, but as long as they stood together, Rishab believed they could overcome even the darkest of battles.

Chapter 13

New Alarm, New Threats

The atmosphere in the **Chirayu Foundation's command center** buzzed with nervous energy, each pulse of the machinery reflecting the collective anxiety of its operators. The room was a sanctuary of both cutting-edge technology and ancient wisdom, where the fate of time and the universe hung precariously on data streams and the movements of their enemies. Today, however, the usual hum had given way to a deafening siren—the sound of an urgent new threat.

Red lights flashed across the room, reflecting off the metallic surfaces and casting the entire team in an ominous glow. Screens flickered rapidly, displaying maps with glowing red markers that signified danger—danger that was unfolding faster than they could act.

At the edge of the command room stood **Rishab**, his eyes locked on the screen, sharp and unwavering. He had no time for doubt or fear; his mind was already working through strategies, potential outcomes, and the ever-present threat of **Moksha**. Roshan was still in recovery, but his fighting spirit had not dimmed. **Reet** was nearby, her fingers dancing across a console as she rapidly processed the incoming intelligence. Indra stood at the center of the room, commanding the attention of everyone present.

The air was thick with anticipation as the alarm blared louder, signaling the gravity of the situation.

Indra (cutting through the noise with a commanding voice): "Quiet! Full briefing, now! What's happening?"

An analyst at one of the main consoles turned to face him, her face pale with urgency. She spoke quickly, knowing the weight of the words she carried.

Analyst (nervously but with focus): "Intel just came in from our field agents. Moksha's forces have been sighted heading toward three separate locations—each tied to ancient weapons of unimaginable power. He's making his move, sir."

Her words landed like a hammer blow, and the entire room seemed to freeze for a moment. Rishab's heart pounded as the realization set in. **Three locations**. Three weapons. These weren't just any artifacts; they were ancient tools of war capable of reshaping reality itself. The idea of Moksha possessing even one of them was terrifying enough, but if he managed to secure all three…

Reet's eyes darted to the screen, her mind already working at lightning speed. She scanned the maps that glowed ominously before them—red dots marking the locations of these powerful relics. The tension in the room thickened as the reality of what they were up against settled over everyone like a heavy fog.

Indra's face hardened as he processed the information. His usual stoic demeanor gave way to visible concern, and his voice, while calm, was underpinned with urgency.

Indra (grimly but with authority): "We can't let Moksha get his hands on these weapons. If he manages to gather even one more of them, it will tip the balance of power completely in his favor. These weapons aren't just relics—they're tied to forces older than time itself. Forces we've barely begun to understand. If he controls them, he'll control everything. He could rewrite history."

The weight of Indra's words pressed down on them like the gravity of a collapsing star. **Moksha** already had one weapon, which had tipped the scales dangerously in his favor. If he gained access to these additional weapons—tools that even the gods themselves had used in the most ancient of wars—their fight against him would become nearly impossible.

Rishab clenched his fists at his sides, the sense of dread in his stomach twisting into a tight knot. He had faced **Moksha** many times before, across lifetimes, and he had always managed to stop him. But this time felt different. **Moksha** was relentless, smarter than ever, and his forces were no longer bound by the limitations of time or space. They were racing against a ticking clock, and the seconds were slipping away.

Rishab (his voice steady but filled with urgency): "Where are these weapons located? We need to move now, before Moksha gains any more ground."

Indra gestured toward the holographic map, which flickered to display three red marks in different corners of the world. These were no ordinary locations—they were places protected by ancient magic, hidden by the gods themselves to prevent them from falling into the wrong hands. But now, **Moksha's forces** were closing in on them.

Indra (gesturing to the map, his tone sharp): "The first location is a spear—once wielded by a god. It's hidden in the high mountains of the north, and it has the power to channel lightning and storms. The second is a shield, buried deep in the jungle ruins of an ancient temple. This shield can absorb and redirect any form of energy thrown at it, making its wielder nearly invulnerable. The third…"

(Indra hereettes, his brow furrowing before he continues.)

"We don't have all the intel on the third yet, but it's rumored to be a sword—a blade that can cut through the very fabric of time itself."

The silence in the room deepened as everyone digested the magnitude of what they were hearing. Each of these weapons was capable of catastrophic destruction on its own. Together, they could grant **Moksha** the ability to bend the entire universe to his will.

Reet (her voice measured but urgent): "Three locations, and we don't have the manpower to cover them all at once. We'll need to split up and move fast. If we waste any time, Moksha will have his hands on these weapons before we can blink."

Rishab nodded, his mind racing as he formulated a plan. Splitting up would be dangerous, but they had no other choice. Moksha's forces were vast, and they were growing stronger with each passing day. The thought of facing another battle so soon after Roshan's close brush with death made Rishab uneasy, but time was not on their side.

Rishab (resolute but thoughtful): "We can't wait any longer. We have to stop Moksha before he reaches those weapons."

Indra's sharp gaze swept across the room before landing back on Rishab and the team.

Indra (firmly, his voice filled with the gravity of their mission): "We'll divide into teams. Rishab, you'll take Roshan and head for the spear in the north. Reet, you'll lead the team to the shield in the jungle. I'll mobilize what remains of our forces to gather intel on the third weapon's location. We can't afford any mistakes."

Rishab's brow furrowed as he heard Indra's plan. **Roshan** was still recovering from his near-fatal injuries, and the thought of sending him back into the field so soon filled Rishab with unease. Roshan was strong—he had proven that time and time again—but he was still human, and Rishab couldn't help but feel protective.

Rishab (hereetnt, concern lacing his voice): "Roshan's not fully recovered yet. Are we sure he's ready for this?"

Indra's expression softened momentarily, recognizing Rishab's worry. But his resolve remained unshaken. The situation was too dire to wait. Every second counted, and **Moksha** wouldn't hereette to take advantage of their hereettion.

Indra (with resolve): "There's no time to wait, Rishab. Roshan will have to push through. We need every advantage we can get—and that includes him."

The reality of the situation settled over Rishab like a heavy weight. He knew Indra was right—they couldn't afford to leave anyone behind. But Roshan had barely escaped death once, and sending him back into battle felt like tempting fate. Yet, Rishab also knew that this was a fight for more than just their lives—it was a fight for the survival of the world itself.

Sensing the tension in Rishab, **Reet** stepped forward, placing a reassuring hand on his shoulder.

Reet (softly but with determination): "Roshan will be okay, Rishab. He's a fighter—he won't let this stop him. We're all in this together, and we all have to give everything we've got."

Rishab took a deep breath, pushing aside his worry. He had to trust in Roshan's strength. They didn't have the luxury of doubt or fear. The stakes were too high.

Rishab (his voice steady, his mind focused): "Alright. We move now. No hereettion."

Indra nodded, his expression hardening as he prepared to send them out into the fray once more. The entire room seemed to hold its breath as the mission became clear. They were walking into another fight with **Moksha's forces**, but this time, the stakes were higher than ever before. They weren't just battling for survival—they were battling for control of the very forces that governed time and space.

Indra (with authority, his gaze sweeping over the team): "Stay alert. Moksha's forces will stop at nothing to secure these weapons, and they won't be fighting fair. You all know what's at stake. If Moksha gains even one more of those weapons, our fight becomes infinitely harder. These aren't just relics—they're keys to controlling everything."

The room buzzed with a palpable tension as everyone prepared to set out on their respective missions. **Roshan**, still pale but determined, arrived from the infirmary, leaning slightly on his staff for support. His steps were unsteady, but the fire in his eyes was as strong as ever.

Roshan (gritting his teeth, his voice rough but resolute): "I'm not sitting this one out. Let's go."

Rishab couldn't help but feel a mixture of pride and concern for his brother-in-arms. Roshan had always been fierce, but this fight had pushed them all to their limits. Rishab only hoped that they could make it through without losing anyone else.

Rishab (in thought, his determination strengthening): We're heading into dangerous territory, but we don't have a choice. Moksha's gaining ground, and we can't let him win.

With a final glance at the screens displaying the locations of the ancient weapons, the team began to move. The weight of the mission hung heavily over them all, but they pushed forward, their resolve unwavering.

As they left the command center and stepped out into the cold night air, the world seemed to shift around them. The future was uncertain, and the threat of **Moksha** loomed larger than ever. But despite the fear and the danger, Rishab knew one thing for sure—they wouldn't stop fighting. Not now. Not ever.

The fate of time itself rested on their next moves.

Chapter 14

Blueprints of War

The air inside the **Chirayu Foundation's command center** buzzed with an electric tension. The room was alive with the hum of machinery, the flicker of holographic screens displaying maps, schematics, and flashing red alerts marking Moksha's growing influence. The anticipation of battle surged through every member of the team as they prepared for what could very well be their final confrontation. Today was not just another mission. This was a battle for the future—quite literally.

Rishab stood apart from the others, deep in thought, as his eyes scanned the map projected before him. It showed three glowing red dots, each representing the ancient weapons that Moksha sought: a godly spear hidden in the mountains, a shield that could absorb any force deep in the jungle, and a sword rumored to cut through the fabric of time itself, buried beneath desert sands. These were no ordinary relics. They were weapons of catastrophic power, capable of reshaping reality, and in the wrong hands, they could destroy the very fabric of time.

Rishab's mind raced. His heart pounded with a mixture of dread and responsibility. The fight ahead would be unlike anything they had faced. **Roshan** and **Reet** were already preparing, gearing up in the armory as they double-checked their equipment. The Foundation's advanced technology—a blend of cutting-edge science and ancient mystical artifacts—was their only advantage against Moksha's forces. But would it be enough?

Rishab (in thought, deeply conflicted):

Every battle before this has led to this moment. But this time... what if I can't stop him?

Roshan, who was still recovering from his near-fatal injuries, refused to slow down. He was already fastening his armor, testing the weight of his staff, his face a mask of determination. The exhaustion was evident in his movements, but his spirit had not dimmed. He had the heart of a warrior, and he wasn't about to let anything—wounds or otherwise—stop him.

Roshan (gruffly, full of resolve): "I don't care how many times Moksha's had the upper hand. This time, we end it."

Rishab, who had been pacing, paused to look at Roshan. His brother-in-arms was pushing himself too hard, but Rishab knew better than to suggest Roshan sit this one out. They had been through too much together—fought side by side in battles that seemed hopeless, yet always finding a way to win. This was no different. But the weight of leadership pressed down on Rishab's shoulders. He had to protect them all—Roshan, Reet, and the rest of the team. If they failed today, it wouldn't just be their lives lost. It would be the world, the very flow of time.

Across the room, Reet was busy fine-tuning the advanced tech she would take into battle. Her hands moved deftly, adjusting the settings on her wrist-mounted device, which allowed her to interact with the energy fields surrounding the ancient relics. Her brilliant mind, always calculating, was already anticipating the traps and defenses they would face. She glanced up from her work, her sharp eyes locking with Rishab's.

Reet (focused but calm, trying to ease Rishab's tension): "Each of these locations will be heavily guarded, not just by Moksha's forces, but by the traps left to protect the weapons. We can't afford any mistakes. We need to move carefully and with precision."

Rishab nodded, but his mind was still swirling with thoughts of the impending battle. His gaze drifted to the map again, the three red dots glowing ominously against the digital landscape. The spear, the shield, and the sword—each capable of unleashing unimaginable destruction. If Moksha managed to get his hands on all three, it wouldn't just be the end of their world. It would be the end of history as they knew it.

Rishab (in thought, a cold knot forming in his gut): *If we fail... Moksha won't just win this battle. He'll rewrite history, reshape the future.*

As if sensing his unease, Reet moved closer to him. Her voice was soft but firm, carrying the confidence that Rishab was struggling to summon.

Reet (with quiet determination): "Rishab, we're ready for this. You've led us this far. We trust you. Don't let doubt cloud your mind now."

Rishab met her gaze, grateful for her words, but the doubt lingered. He had always been the one to carry the burden of leadership, the one who had to make the hard choices. But now, with **Moksha** growing stronger, with these ancient weapons capable of so much destruction in play, the stakes felt impossibly high. His heart beat faster with every passing second.

Rishab (softly, voicing his fears): "It's just... Moksha has grown stronger. The weapons, the forces he's gathering—they're more powerful than anything we've faced before. If he gets them..."

Before Rishab could finish, Roshan's voice cut through the air, sharp and fierce. He had overheard the conversation and wasn't about to let doubt creep into the room.

Roshan (with conviction, fire in his eyes): "Moksha's been powerful in every lifetime, Rishab. And we've stopped him in every single one. We're not going to lose now—not after everything we've been through."

There was something about Roshan's raw determination that always managed to cut through Rishab's doubt. Even as he battled his own injuries, Roshan's spirit remained unbroken. He was a fighter, through and through. Rishab gave a small nod, feeling the familiar weight of responsibility settle over him once more. They had faced Moksha before. They had stopped him before. They could do it again—but this time, they needed to be smarter.

Rishab (resolute, his voice steady): "You're right. We've stopped him before, and we'll do it again. But this time, no recklessness. No mistakes."

Roshan's lips curved into a small grin, though the exhaustion was still evident in his eyes.

Roshan (with a hint of humor): "Don't worry about me, Rishab. I've still got plenty of fight left."

Reet finished adjusting her gear and joined them, her expression calm but determined.

Reet (with quiet confidence): "We've got a plan. Let's stick to it. The traps, the weapons, whatever Moksha's forces throw at us—we're ready."

Rishab looked between his two closest allies, feeling a renewed sense of purpose settle over him. Despite the immense danger they were walking into, they had each other. That was what had kept them alive this long. That was what would keep them going.

With their gear prepared, the three of them made their way to the command center for a final briefing. The holographic map of the world spread out before them, showing the three key locations they needed to reach: the high mountains where the spear was hidden, the dense jungle ruins guarding the shield, and the desolate desert plains where the sword was sealed.

Indra stood at the head of the table, his expression grim. He had been through countless battles, seen enemies rise and fall, but this... this was something else entirely. As he looked at the team, he knew that what lay ahead would test them like never before.

Indra (urgently, his voice commanding): "Remember, these aren't just weapons—they're artifacts of immense power. Moksha won't be the only obstacle. The guardians of these places won't give up their secrets easily. You'll face magical traps, ancient defenses, and Moksha's forces. Stay sharp and trust each other."

The room was silent as the team processed the gravity of what was ahead. Rishab felt the weight of the mission press down on him, but he knew they had no other choice. If they didn't act now, Moksha would gain the upper hand, and there would be no stopping him.

Rishab (addressing the team with newfound resolve): "We've faced Moksha before. We know what he's capable of, but he doesn't know what we've become. We fight together, and we stop him here. Let's move."

The team dispersed, heading toward their individual missions with a sense of quiet determination. As Rishab, Roshan, and Reet set off for the mountains, the anticipation of battle thrummed in the air around them. The weight of time itself hung heavy on their shoulders, but they were ready.

As they made their way into the misty landscape beyond the Foundation, the ground beneath them seemed to pulse with ancient energy. Every step they took was a step closer to confronting the most dangerous force they had ever encountered. Rishab's heart pounded in his chest, but his mind was clear. They had faced Moksha before, and they would face him again.

The mist thickened as they approached the base of the mountain, the peaks looming ominously above them. In the distance, they could hear the faint sound of something stirring—**Moksha's forces**, already in position. The battle ahead would be fierce, but Rishab knew that they had no other choice. They had to win. For Roshan, for Reet, for the future.

Rishab (in thought, as the battle loomed ahead): *No matter the cost, we have to win.*

The stage was set. The battle for the future, for time itself, was about to begin.

Chapter 15

The Hour of Reckoning

The battleground was a vast and ancient land where the past and future collided. The swirling mist seemed to pulse with an otherworldly energy, shrouding the jagged ruins and hidden weapons that could reshape time itself. Rishab, Roshan, Reet, and Indra moved through the haze, their every step weighed down by the enormity of the task ahead. Somewhere beyond the mist, Moksha's forces were already on the move, relentlessly pursuing the three legendary weapons—the spear, the shield, and the sword—that could grant Moksha the power to rewrite the past and seize control of the future.

The four of them were hardened by battle, but the stakes had never been higher. Roshan's injuries from their last skirmish hadn't fully healed, but he refused to be sidelined. His fierce spirit burned as brightly as ever, but Rishab could see the tension in his brother's eyes. Reet, ever the strategist, had studied the ancient texts and maps, her keen intellect guiding them through the treacherous traps that lay ahead. And Indra, the seasoned leader of the Chirayu Foundation, radiated a calm, focused authority as he prepared the team for the greatest battle they had ever faced.

But for Rishab, the weight of leadership had never been heavier. Every decision, every moment of hereettion, could be the difference between saving time and watching it unravel. The three weapons, hidden across treacherous landscapes, were the last pieces Moksha needed to complete his plan. If he succeeded, the future would be lost.

Indra (voice steady, but urgent): "Stay sharp. Moksha's forces are ahead. They'll be desperate now—this is their last chance to tip the scales in their favor."

Rishab gave a quick nod, though his mind raced with thoughts of the battle to come. They had fought Moksha and his minions before, but this time, it felt different. Stronger. More dangerous. The very air around them seemed to vibrate with an unseen force, as if the land itself understood the gravity of what was unfolding.

Rishab (in thought, tense and focused): *We've fought through everything Moksha has thrown at us, but this... This feels different. He knows what's at stake, and he's ready.*

As they pushed forward, the mist parted slightly, revealing the first line of Moksha's forces—his soldiers were a deadly combination of ancient warriors, their bodies enhanced with futuristic technology. They wore armor that shimmered with a dark energy, and their weapons crackled with power from both the past and the future. The clash of timelines was palpable, and the tension on the battlefield thickened with every passing second.

The team split up according to their plan. Reet, with her deep knowledge of the traps and defenses that guarded the weapons, headed for the underground chamber where the spear lay hidden. Rishab, Roshan, and Indra prepared to hold off Moksha's forces, buying Reet the time she needed to retrieve the weapon.

Roshan, despite his injuries, charged into battle without hereettion. His staff spun in furious arcs as he tore through the soldiers in his path. Every strike was fueled by his raw determination, his need to fight through the pain, to make sure that this time, Moksha's forces wouldn't win.

Roshan (shouting through gritted teeth, voice full of fury): "I don't care how many they send! We're not letting them win this time!"

Rishab followed closely behind, moving with a deadly precision that had been honed through countless battles. His time-jumping abilities gave him an advantage as he blinked in and out of the present, dodging attacks and delivering devastating blows before the enemy even knew where he was. Indra, calm and disciplined, fought with the precision of a seasoned warrior. His sword hummed with energy as he parried incoming blasts and countered with brutal efficiency, cutting down the enemies that dared approach him.

Rishab (shouting to Indra, breath quick from the fight): "We need to give Reet more time! Keep them off her!"

Indra nodded without breaking stride, his sword deflecting a blast of energy aimed directly at Rishab. The battlefield was a whirlwind of chaos—enemy soldiers surged forward in waves, their numbers seemingly endless. Every step forward felt like an uphill battle, but the team held their ground. Still, a gnawing sense of unease tugged at the edge of Rishab's mind. There were too many enemies. More than they had anticipated.

Rishab's heart sank as he realized what was happening. Through the thick of the fight, he caught sight of one of Moksha's scientists, cloaked in futuristic armor, standing behind the lines of soldiers. The scientist wasn't engaged in the battle. Instead, he was working at a console, his fingers flying over the controls. In front of him, a massive cloning device whirred to life, pumping out a seemingly endless stream of Moksha's fallen henchmen. Every time one was cut down, another rose to take its place.

Rishab (urgently, voice cutting through the noise of battle as he called out to Indra): "They're cloning the henchmen! If we don't stop that scientist, we'll be overwhelmed!"

Roshan, hearing the conversation, roared in frustration. His eyes blazed with anger as he charged through the waves of soldiers, his staff spinning wildly as he cut through them, his body a blur of motion. He fought with a ferocity that bordered on reckless, his fury driving him forward.

Roshan (gritting his teeth, voice raw with determination): "I'll smash that machine into pieces!"

Rishab sprinted alongside him, using his time-jumping to slip between the enemies and dodge their attacks. The battlefield was a blur of flashing lights, energy blasts, and the sound of metal on metal. But Rishab's focus was locked on the scientist and the cloning device. They had to destroy it, or they would be drowned in an endless wave of enemies.

Roshan, his face twisted in anger, leaped toward the device, bringing his staff crashing down with all his might. The machine sparked and whirred before shattering into pieces, sending a shower of sparks into the air. The scientist, eyes wide with panic, stumbled backward, trying to flee, but Roshan's next strike sent him flying into the ruins, his body crumpling against the stone walls. The relentless wave of cloned henchmen came to an abrupt halt, and for a moment, the battlefield fell into a tense, eerie silence.

Indra (calling out from across the field, voice loud and clear): "Good work! But it's not over yet!"

Rishab barely had a moment to catch his breath before the ground shook beneath their feet. From the depths of the battleground, an enormous figure emerged, his footsteps heavy and slow. One of Moksha's most dangerous henchmen—an elite soldier known as **K.A.L-13 (Kill All Life – 13)**—stepped into the fray. He was a monstrous figure, towering over the battlefield in a suit of ancient, enchanted armor that crackled with dark energy. His massive sword, nearly the size of a man, hummed with a malevolent power as he swung it through the air with terrifying speed.

The very ground seemed to tremble with each step he took, and the air around him vibrated with the raw power of the dark magic that fueled him. He moved with a speed

Rishab barely had time to react, his heart pounding in his chest as K.A.L-13 charged toward them.

Rishab (shouting to his team, voice strained): "Brace yourselves! He's stronger than anything we've faced before!"

K.A.L-13's first strike came down like a thunderclap, the sheer force of it sending Roshan flying backward, his body skidding across the dirt. Indra barely managed to block the next attack, but the force of the blow knocked him off his feet. Rishab blinked through time, using his abilities to avoid the devastating strikes, but K.A.L-13 was faster than any enemy he had faced before. His attacks seemed to distort the very fabric of time, warping Rishab's sense of reality and making it nearly impossible to predict his next move.

Rishab (in thought, panic rising as he struggled to anticipate the enemy's attacks): *He's using time against us. We need those weapons now!*

As the battle reached its most intense point, Rishab knew they couldn't hold off K.A.L-13 much longer. His strength was overwhelming, his attacks relentless. Every second they delayed was a second closer to defeat. Their only hope lay with Reet. She was their only chance of turning the tide.

Deep within the underground chamber, Reet sprinted through the final stretch of the labyrinthine ruins. Her heart pounded in her chest as she dodged the last of the traps, her eyes fixed on the faint glow at the end of the chamber. The spear—imbued with the power of a storm god—rested on an ancient altar, its energy crackling faintly in the dim light. Her pulse quickened as she reached out, her fingers brushing the cool metal of the weapon.

The moment her hand closed around the spear, the air around her surged with energy. The spear pulsed in her grip, a wave of power radiating from it as it came to life.

Reet (in thought, heart racing): *I've got the spear. Now we stand a chance.*

Her voice came through Rishab's earpiece, a beacon of hope cutting through the chaos.

Reet (urgently, breathless from the exertion): "Rishab, I have the spear! I'm coming to you now!"

Rishab's heart surged with hope. They weren't finished yet. But as he looked back at K.A.L-13, still looming over the battlefield, his sword crackling with dark power, Rishab knew this was only the beginning. The fight was far from over, and the final confrontation with Moksha and his forces was still to come. The outcome of this battle would decide everything—their future, their past, and the fate of time itself.

Chapter 16

When the Sky Fell Silent

The battlefield sprawled before them like a dark, twisted tapestry of time and power. Mist hung thick in the air, swirling with an ominous energy that seemed to cling to everything, making it difficult to see more than a few feet ahead. Rishab, Roshan, Reet, and Indra stood on the edge of the ancient grounds, their hearts heavy with the knowledge that this battle could be their last stand against Moksha. The stakes had never been higher.

All around them, Moksha's forces surged forward in endless waves, a terrifying combination of ancient warriors bolstered by advanced technology from the future. The clash of steel, the hum of energy weapons, and the guttural cries of battle filled the air, each sound a reminder of the relentless power they were up against.

Rishab's heart raced as he time-jumped to dodge an incoming energy blast, his mind whirling with strategies and counterattacks. They had been fighting for hours, but it felt like days. His limbs were heavy, his thoughts clouded by fatigue, and yet he pushed on. Failure was not an option. The three legendary weapons that Moksha sought—the spear, shield, and sword—were the keys to his ultimate plan, and they couldn't let him win.

Roshan, though still wounded from their previous encounter, fought like a man possessed. His staff moved in blurs of motion, cracking against enemies with deadly precision. Every strike came with a roar of anger, his frustration and determination pouring into every swing. Despite his pain, Roshan refused to slow down.

Roshan (gritting his teeth, furious): "I don't care how many they send! I'll break every last one of them!"

His voice cut through the chaos, but Rishab's attention was elsewhere. Through the mist, he could see the waves of enemies parting, and there, in the distance, Moksha's elite henchmen began to close in on Indra. The leader of the Chirayu Foundation had been fighting fiercely, his sword glowing with ancient energy as he cut through enemy after enemy. But now, they were isolating him, driving him away from the rest of the team, creating a deadly trap.

Rishab (shouting, panic rising in his voice): "Indra! They're trying to separate us—get back here!"

But it was too late. Indra was surrounded. The elite henchmen moved with coordinated precision, cutting off his escape routes. Their weapons crackled with dark energy, and they circled him like predators, waiting for the right moment to strike. Rishab's heart pounded in his chest as he saw the trap close around Indra.

Indra fought valiantly, his movements graceful and deadly. He deflected their strikes, parried their attacks, and even in his isolation, he held his own. But Rishab could see the strain on his face. Indra was outnumbered, and the fatigue of battle was starting to take its toll.

Indra (shouting over the noise of battle, voice filled with urgency): "Don't let them take the weapon! We can't lose it!"

Indra's voice carried through the battlefield, cutting through the din of clashing weapons and shouting enemies. But as he spoke, one of Moksha's elite—a towering, armored warrior wielding a massive axe—charged at him. Indra raised his sword to block the strike, but the sheer force of the attack knocked him off balance. He stumbled, his footing lost, and in that split second, the rest of Moksha's henchmen closed in.

Rishab (desperately, voice thick with panic): "Indra! Hold on—I'm coming!"

Rishab's feet moved before his mind could catch up. He time-jumped, racing through the battlefield, trying to close the distance between him and Indra. But it was like moving through quicksand. For every step forward, another wave of enemies crashed into him, slowing him down, pulling him away. He saw Roshan fighting to reach Indra as well, but more of Moksha's soldiers blocked his path, their weapons slashing through the air with deadly intent.

Roshan fought furiously, his staff whirling in wide arcs, knocking enemies back with every strike. His face was contorted with rage, and though his body was weakened by his injuries, he pushed forward with pure adrenaline. But even Roshan, with all his strength, couldn't break through fast enough.

Roshan (roaring in frustration, voice filled with fury): "We need to get to him! They're closing in!"

Reet, clutching the ancient spear she had recovered, sprinted toward Rishab, her eyes wide with fear. She could see what was happening—Indra was being overwhelmed, and Moksha's forces were after the weapon he held. If they captured it, everything would be lost.

Reet (breathless, voice tight with fear): "Rishab! They're after Indra's weapon—if they get it, it's over!"

Through the smoke and chaos, Rishab saw the inevitable unfold. The towering henchman, his axe glowing with dark energy, lunged at Indra again. This time, Indra's sword slipped from his grasp, clattering to the ground with a sound that cut through the chaos like a death knell. The weapon, the last piece Moksha needed to complete his plan, lay at the feet of the enemy.

Indra (gasping, trying to rally his strength, voice filled with urgency): "Stay focused! Don't let them—!"

But his voice was drowned out by the roar of the battle. The elite henchmen pressed in, and before Rishab could reach him, the final blow landed. The massive henchman swung his axe in a wide arc, and it crashed into Indra's side with a sickening thud. Indra's body crumpled to the ground, blood splattering across the dirt as the force of the strike sent him to his knees.

Time seemed to slow as Rishab watched in horror, helpless to intervene. He was too far away, too slow to stop what was happening. Indra, the seasoned leader, the man who had guided them through every battle, fell to the ground, his body battered and broken.

Rishab (in thought, panic flooding his mind):

No... this can't be happening.

The elite henchmen moved quickly, grabbing Indra's fallen weapon—the last piece Moksha needed to complete his dark plan. The air around the weapon crackled with malevolent energy, and as soon as it was in their grasp, the entire battlefield seemed to grow darker, heavier, as if the very air had been poisoned by the power of the weapon.

Reet (desperately, voice filled with disbelief): "Rishab, we have to stop them! We can't let them take it!"

But Rishab's body felt frozen, his mind screaming at him to act, to fight, but his limbs refusing to move. The battlefield was slipping from their control. Roshan was still fighting with everything he had, but he too was being pushed back. The endless waves of enemies were closing in on all sides, and without Indra's weapon, they had no way to turn the tide.

Rishab (shouting, voice hoarse with frustration): "Indra! Hold on—we're coming!"

But it was too late. Moksha's henchmen dragged Indra's limp form away from the battlefield, their mission accomplished. As they retreated into the mist, the dark energy from the weapon pulsed ominously, signaling that Moksha's plan was now one step closer to completion.

Rishab's heart pounded in his chest, a mix of anger, frustration, and helplessness consuming him. They had come so far, fought so hard, but now—now they were on the verge of losing everything.

The battlefield quieted as the enemies retreated, but the victory was hollow. Rishab's gaze fell on Indra's motionless body, lying in the dirt. The once unshakable leader of the Chirayu Foundation had been defeated, his weapon taken, and with it, their hope of stopping Moksha.

Roshan (furious, voice trembling with rage): "We can't let them get away with this! We have to fight!"

But Rishab knew the truth. They couldn't win without the weapon. The realization hit him like a blow to the chest. Moksha had outmaneuvered them, and now, he held the final piece of the puzzle. His mind raced, searching for a way to salvage what was left, but the harsh reality was unavoidable. They had been outplayed, and the path forward was now darker than ever.

Rishab (whispering, in disbelief): "We've lost…"

Reet knelt beside Indra's fallen body, her face pale, her hands trembling as she checked for a pulse. There was still breath in his chest, but the defeat in his eyes was unmistakable. He had fought valiantly, but now he lay powerless, his weapon gone.

Indra (weakly, voice strained): "Don't… give up. You… can still stop him."

Rishab knelt beside Indra, his heart heavy with guilt and anger. He knew Indra was right—they couldn't stop fighting, not yet. But the weight of the loss felt unbearable. The future, once filled with hope and determination, now seemed uncertain.

Rishab (voice filled with resolve, but tinged with sorrow): “We’ll stop him. We have to.”

But as he spoke, the words felt hollow. The cost of the battle was becoming too much to bear. They had lost Indra’s weapon, and with it, their advantage. The road ahead felt darker and more dangerous than ever before.

The battle wasn’t over—but the cost was becoming unbearable.

Chapter 17

The Engine of Eternity

The underground lab was a fortress of steel and shadows, thrumming with ominous energy. The air vibrated with the chaotic hum of ancient relics entwined with futuristic technology, as the three powerful weapons—Indra's staff, the celestial spear, and the impenetrable shield—glowed fiercely within the conduit. The dark portal at the heart of the machine was already warping the fabric of reality, swirling with menacing energy, as if the boundaries of time and space were crumbling under the strain. The portal was the door through which Moksha would step, fully armed, into the present—a moment that spelled doom for the world as Rishab, Roshan, and Reet knew it.

The scientist, clad in a sleek armored suit that merged the magic of ancient times with technology from the future, moved around the console with maniacal precision. He manipulated holographic controls with fluid movements, his face a mask of gleeful obsession. His eyes flickered with the reflection of the portal's violent energy, his mouth curled into a cruel smirk as he observed the growing instability of the time-bending vortex.

"This is it," the scientist muttered under his breath, fingers flying over the controls. "Moksha will step through, and the future will be rewritten."

Far below, hidden in the shadows near the entrance of the lab, Rishab, Roshan, and Reet crouched behind a cluster of machinery, their eyes locked on the scene unfolding before them. The weight of failure hung heavy in the air—they had already lost Indra, and with him, the final weapon Moksha needed. Now, their only hope was to destroy the machine and stop Moksha's arrival before it was too late.

Reet (whispering, her voice filled with urgency):

"We don't have much time. The portal's stabilizing—it'll be open any minute. Once Moksha steps through, we won't stand a chance."

Rishab's heart pounded as he assessed the situation. The dark energy radiating from the portal was nearly unbearable, and the entire lab was fortified with layers of defense mechanisms—automated turrets armed with deadly energy blasts, glowing energy barriers, and an intricate web of traps designed to prevent any interference. The atmosphere was suffocating, oppressive, as if the very air was thick with the weight of the ancient relics being forced into this unnatural fusion of time and space.

Roshan (gritting his teeth, frustration boiling just below the surface):

"We can't wait any longer. We have to destroy that machine now, or we're finished!"

Rishab shook his head, his mind racing as he scanned the defenses. Charging in blindly would be suicide. The scientist was too well-prepared, the defenses too deadly. They needed a plan—one that could get them past the turrets, through the energy barriers, and to the heart of the machine.

Rishab (with measured determination):

"I'll use the time-jump to bypass the defenses. Reet, you disable the security systems from here. Roshan, once we breach the portal, you're going to have to hit it hard. We need to take this whole thing down in one blow."

The scientist's cold laughter echoed through the lab as he continued working, oblivious to the heroes hidden in the shadows. His voice was filled with arrogance, a deep belief that his victory was inevitable.

Scientist (sneering as he watched the portal stabilize): "You're too late, anyway. The moment Moksha steps through, this world will fall. Time itself will bend to our will, and you? You'll be nothing but relics of a forgotten era."

Rishab's jaw tightened. The scientist's words cut through the heavy air like a blade, but Rishab couldn't afford to let them get to him. He glanced at Roshan, whose fists were clenched so tightly that his knuckles had gone white, and at Reet, who was already scanning the security system, her fingers hovering over her devices.

Rishab (gritting his teeth, voice filled with conviction):

"I'll stop him."

With a deep breath, Rishab activated the chip implanted in his chest. Time began to slow around him, the whirring of machinery and the crackling of energy fading into the background as he entered the heightened state that allowed him to manipulate the flow of time. The world around him became a blur, the beams of deadly energy from the turrets and the bright glow of the barriers shifting into slow motion as Rishab began to move.

He darted forward, dodging between the energy beams with near-inhuman precision. His past lives flashed before his eyes as he wove through the chaos—the memories of countless battles fought against Moksha across the ages, each one shaping him into the warrior he was now. His instincts were honed to a razor's edge, guiding his movements as he pushed closer to the heart of the machine.

As Rishab neared the core, the conduits feeding the ancient weapons' energy into the portal crackled with unstable power. The stolen relics pulsed violently, their mystical energy being siphoned against their will, and Rishab could feel the tension in the air as the portal neared its completion.

Rishab (in thought, determination coursing through him):

This is it. I have to stop this. No more failures.

Rishab reached out, gripping the nearest conduit with both hands and yanking it free. Sparks erupted from the machine as the power flow was disrupted, sending the portal into a violent fit of instability. The dark energy swirling within it faltered for a moment, and the scientist's smug grin disappeared, replaced by wide-eyed panic as he rushed toward the console to stabilize the system.

Scientist (shouting in panic, fear creeping into his voice):

"No! What are you doing?! You can't possibly understand the forces you're meddling with!"

But Rishab wasn't finished. He moved with precision, tearing away another conduit, causing the entire lab to tremble as the machine sputtered and the portal wavered. Dark energy crackled through the air, lashing out like a wild beast as the power from the ancient weapons was severed.

Reet (from behind, focused on disabling the defenses):

"Keep going, Rishab! The security system is almost down—I'm deactivating the turrets now!"

Roshan, watching Rishab from across the room, could barely contain his frustration. He wanted nothing more than to charge forward and destroy the machine himself, but he knew that Rishab was their best chance of reaching the core without being incinerated by the defenses. His knuckles whitened around the hilt of his staff as he prepared to strike the moment the barriers came down.

But just as it seemed they were gaining ground, the entire room shook violently. The scientist slammed his hand down on the console, unleashing a surge of dark energy that ripped through the lab. Rishab was thrown backward by the force of the blast, crashing into a wall with enough impact to leave him gasping for breath.

Rishab (struggling to rise, the pain coursing through him):

"No… I have to stop it…"

As Rishab pushed himself to his feet, his vision blurry from the impact, the dark energy from the portal surged once more. The machine roared back to life, the portal stabilizing with a ferocity that sent shockwaves through the room. The air grew thick with malevolence, the swirling mass of dark energy taking shape as a figure began to emerge from its depths.

Moksha had arrived.

Chapter 18

The Arrival of the False God

The swirling chaos of the portal filled the lab with an oppressive pressure, making it difficult to breathe. As Rishab struggled to his feet, the sound of crackling energy and the hum of the machine reached a deafening crescendo. His body ached from the earlier blast, but his eyes were locked on the figure stepping through the portal.

Moksha emerged from the vortex like a dark god, his form cloaked in swirling energy that bent reality around him. His eyes glowed with a malevolent power that sent a chill down Rishab's spine, and the air itself seemed to warp and twist in his presence. Behind him, an endless tide of cloned soldiers marched through the portal, their faces blank and lifeless, their movements synchronized with mechanical precision.

The sheer force of Moksha's presence was overwhelming. The ground beneath him cracked and splintered, and the stolen relics—the celestial spear, Indra's staff, and the shield—pulsed in unison with his arrival, resonating with the dark energy that now controlled them. His smile was cruel, his gaze filled with triumph as he surveyed the battlefield before him.

Moksha (with a wicked smile, his voice dripping with arrogance):

"Did you really think you could stop me, Rishab? Time bends to my will now. You and your pathetic allies are nothing more than relics of the past, standing in the way of progress."

Reet, Roshan, and Rishab stood frozen for a moment, the weight of Moksha's presence pressing down on them like a suffocating blanket. The power radiating from him was unlike anything they had encountered before—an unnatural force that distorted reality itself. Rishab's heart pounded in his chest, his mind racing as he tried to find a way to fight back.

But how could they defeat someone who controlled time itself?

Roshan (gritting his teeth, his voice filled with defiance):

"I don't care how powerful you are, Moksha! We're not backing down now!"

Without hereettion, Roshan charged into the fray, his staff swinging with fury as he cut through the wave of clones. Each strike was precise, fueled by the rage bubbling beneath his surface, but no matter how many enemies he felled, more kept pouring through the portal.

Reet, her mind sharp and focused, moved beside Roshan, using the spear she had retrieved to strike down enemies with calculated precision. But even she could feel the weight of the battle turning against them. The clones were relentless, and Moksha's mere presence was warping the battlefield into a twisted nightmare.

Moksha hovered above them, his arms outstretched as if relishing the chaos. His laughter echoed through the lab, cold and mocking.

Moksha (mockingly, his voice filled with contempt):

"Naive fools. Do you really think you can defeat me now? I control time, and I control your fate."

Rishab, still reeling from the earlier blast, forced himself to focus. His body was battered, but his mind was racing. He couldn't let Moksha win—not like this. The memories of his past lives surged through him, battles fought across centuries, victories and losses that had shaped him into the warrior he was now. But this… this was different. Moksha was stronger than ever before, and with the stolen relics, he had become a godlike force.

Rishab (in thought, struggling to remain composed):

He's using time against us. We need those weapons.

The battle raged on, but it was becoming clear that they were losing ground. The sheer number of clones, combined with the overwhelming presence of Moksha, made every step forward feel like an impossible task. For every enemy they defeated, ten more took their place.

And then, without warning, Moksha made his move.

With a flick of his wrist, Moksha summoned a spear of dark energy from the portal. The weapon crackled with malevolent power, its very presence distorting the air around it. His eyes locked onto Rishab, and with a sinister grin, he hurled the spear toward him with terrifying speed.

Moksha (laughing, his voice filled with malice):

"Let's see if your past lives can save you now, Rishab."

The spear tore through the air with deadly accuracy, and before Rishab could react, it struck him directly in the chest. The force of the blow was devastating, sending shockwaves through his body. Rishab staggered, his breath catching in his throat as the dark energy from the spear coursed through him, searing his flesh and warping his mind.

Pain surged through his body as he collapsed to the ground, gasping for air, his vision blurring as darkness crept in.

Roshan (shouting in horror, voice raw with desperation):

"RISHAB!"

Reet (her voice shaking, disbelief in her eyes):

"No… this can't be happening…"

As Rishab lay on the ground, his body wracked with pain, Moksha descended toward him, his eyes gleaming with cruel satisfaction. But Moksha wasn't alone. From the swirling chaos of the portal, another figure emerged—a young man cloaked in shadows, radiating the same dark energy that surrounded Moksha.

The sight of him sent a shockwave through the battlefield. Rishab's heart pounded in his chest, though weakened from the spear's blow, as he struggled to comprehend what he was seeing. The young man stepped forward, his face cold and expressionless, his eyes devoid of any emotion.

Moksha (grinning, voice cold and filled with triumph):

"Meet your son, Rishab. He carries your power... and he will be my greatest weapon."

Rishab's mind reeled as he looked at the young man standing beside Moksha. His son? How could this be? How had Moksha twisted the future to bring forth this dark version of his own blood?

Rishab (weakly, voice trembling with disbelief):

"My son… how?"

But there was no time for answers. The cold, emotionless eyes of Rishab's son bore into him, and Moksha's cruel laughter filled the room.

Moksha (with satisfaction, his voice dripping with venom):

"Your son is mine, Rishab. You have failed, and now he will help me bring this world to its knees."

Roshan and Reet could only watch in stunned horror as Rishab lay on the brink of death, the dark spear still embedded in his chest, his life slipping away. Moksha, the scientist, and Rishab's son now stood victorious, their plan nearly complete. The portal continued to roar with dark energy, a gateway to an apocalyptic future.

Scientist (laughing maniacally, drunk on power):

"It's over. The weapons, the portal, everything is ours!"

With a final, triumphant laugh, Moksha, the scientist, and Rishab's son turned away from the fallen heroes. They disappeared through the portal, leaving destruction in their wake. The lab fell into a haunting silence, broken only by the sound of Rishab's labored breathing as he lay dying on the cold ground.

Roshan and Reet rushed to his side, their hearts pounding with fear and disbelief.

Chapter 19

The Spear and the Soul

The laboratory was eerily silent now, a hollow stillness settling in the space where chaos had raged moments before. The shadows flickered and pulsed as if echoing the dark energy that had just torn through their ranks. Roshan and Reet stood at the threshold of the devastation, their faces a blend of terror and disbelief. Moksha had gone, but he had left a nightmare in his wake.

Rishab lay sprawled on the cold metal floor, the dark spear lodged in his chest pulsing with a sinister energy. Each throb of the weapon seemed to drain the life from him, its dark energy casting twisted shadows across his face. Roshan stumbled toward him, his footsteps heavy and frantic, while Reet knelt beside Rishab, her face lined with shock and grief.

Roshan (desperate, voice trembling):

"Rishab... Rishab! Don't you dare leave us. Don't you dare!"

Rishab's chest rose and fell in shallow, labored breaths, each inhale weaker than the last. His vision blurred as he blinked up at Reet and Roshan, but he could barely see them. The darkness was creeping in, wrapping around him, blurring the edges of reality. It was like a black tide, threatening to pull him under.

Reet's hands found his, gripping them tightly. Her usually calm and composed face was a mask of raw emotion, her eyes shining with unshed tears.

Reet (whispering, voice breaking):

"Rishab… stay with us. Don't leave me. Don't leave us…"

Rishab's lips curved in a faint, pained smile, his gaze softening as he looked at her, his best friend, his confidante, the one who had been by his side through every lifetime. He fought to stay conscious, to hold onto her voice, to anchor himself to the present. But the spear pulsed, and the dark energy surged, pulling him deeper into the void.

Rishab (struggling to speak):

"Reet… Roshan… I… I thought I'd… be strong enough."

Roshan (voice choked with rage and sorrow):

"You are strong enough, Rishab! You always have been. We've always fought through everything together."

Rishab's gaze shifted, focusing on Roshan, his friend, his brother in all but blood. Roshan's face was a mixture of anger and helplessness, his fists clenched as though sheer will alone could reverse the inevitable.

Rishab (whispering, pained):

"You have to... carry on. No matter what."

Roshan shook his head fiercely, unwilling to accept it. He dropped to his knees, gripping Rishab's shoulder as if he could hold him back from the brink of death.

Roshan (desperate):

"No! We're not giving up on you, Rishab. You'll come through this. You always do!"

But as Rishab looked into their faces, a flicker of peace passed over him. He had fought so many battles, defied death across lifetimes. He had been the warrior, the strategist, the protector. And now... he felt the cold embrace of defeat. He had never been able to save everyone. And he had failed this time too.

The spear pulsed again, darkness flooding his senses, and he gasped as agony surged through him. Reet's grip tightened, her voice desperate, filled with a pleading urgency.

Reet (whispering, voice breaking):

"Don't leave us, Rishab. You're stronger than this. You're the only one who can stop Moksha… you're the only one."

A flicker of anguish crossed Rishab's face, his eyes glassy as he tried to focus on her face, to anchor himself. But his strength was fading. His mind was slipping away, and all he could hear was the distant echo of Moksha's laughter, cold and triumphant, resonating in his mind.

In his final moments of consciousness, a memory surfaced—a vision of the son he had seen standing beside Moksha, a twisted reflection of himself. His son, who bore the power he had once hoped to use for good, now manipulated by Moksha. A wave of grief washed over him, more painful than any physical wound. How had it come to this? How had Moksha managed to twist his future so irrevocably?

Rishab (whispering, his voice barely audible):

"My son… how… how did this happen?"

But the darkness surged again, and the last thing he saw before slipping into unconsciousness was Reet's tear-streaked face, her lips moving in silent prayer.

As Rishab's eyes drifted closed, Reet fought against the truth that was sinking into her heart. She leaned closer, whispering words of comfort, of hope, even as his breathing grew faint. Her hands were covered in his blood, but she didn't care. She would hold him together if she had to; she would keep him alive through sheer willpower alone.

Reet (pleading):

"Rishab… you can't leave us. You can't leave me…"

The room was heavy with silence, the weight of their grief pressing down like a physical force. The cold air hung thick around them, and every second stretched out, a painful reminder of the fading heartbeat beneath her hands. Roshan stood beside her, silent, his face a mask of despair as he watched the light fade from Rishab's eyes.

A small, soft gasp escaped Rishab, and his chest stilled, his body going limp in her arms.

For a heartbeat, the world held its breath.

Outside, the sky darkened, a storm gathering on the horizon. The wind howled through the broken walls of the lab, as if mourning alongside them. Reet's hands trembled as she clutched Rishab's still form, her mind numb with disbelief. She could feel the emptiness, the hollow ache of loss spreading through her.

Roshan turned away, his fists clenched tightly, his jaw set as he tried to suppress the wave of emotions threatening to overtake him. They had lost. Despite their strength, their courage, they had lost.

Roshan (whispering, voice breaking):

"No… Rishab… you can't be gone."

A tear slipped down his face, unbidden, and he angrily wiped it away, a helpless fury building inside him. How could this have happened? How had they let Moksha win? The guilt weighed heavily on him, a crushing burden that seemed to press down on his very soul.

As Reet held Rishab's body, her mind raced, replaying the moments of their battle, the choices they had made, the trust they had placed in him. She refused to accept that he was truly gone. Rishab, who had always risen, always fought back, always survived—this couldn't be the end.

The silence was shattered by a faint, barely perceptible pulse beneath her fingertips. It was faint, like a whisper, but it was there. Her heart leaped, hope flaring like a fragile spark in the darkness.

Reet (in a hushed whisper):

"Rishab…?"

She held her breath, her fingers pressing against his neck, searching for any sign of life. The pulse flickered again, weak but steady, a quiet, stubborn rhythm that seemed to defy the darkness surrounding them. She looked up at Roshan, her eyes wide with a mixture of shock and hope.

Reet (whispering urgently):

"He's alive, Roshan. He's still alive!"

Roshan's head snapped up, his eyes widening as he stared down at Rishab's still form, disbelief and hope battling within him. He dropped to his knees beside her, his hands shaking as he reached out, feeling for himself the faint pulse beneath Rishab's skin.

A flicker of relief crossed his face, and he let out a shaky breath, his voice barely above a whisper.

Roshan (awed, voice choked with emotion):

"Rishab… you're still here."

But Rishab remained unconscious, his breathing shallow, his face pale. They had won a reprieve, a momentary hope, but his life still hung by a thread. The dark energy from the spear continued to seep into him, a slow poison that was claiming him inch by inch.

Reet looked at Roshan, determination hardening her gaze.

Reet (fiercely):

"We can't let him go. We have to save him."

Roshan (resolved):

"We will. Whatever it takes. Rishab's not leaving us. Not now. Not ever."

They lifted him carefully, their movements gentle yet filled with urgency. As they made their way out of the ruined lab, the storm broke, rain pouring down around them, drenching them as if the heavens themselves mourned alongside them.

The path ahead was uncertain, the future dark and unknown.

But as they disappeared into the rain, one question remained, an unanswered echo in the depths of their hearts:

Would Rishab survive? Or had the dark spear already sealed his fate?

The End